Blood on the Tyne

Body Parts

Colin Garrow

A Rosie Robson Murder Mystery

Distributed by Amazon
Copyright © 2020 Colin Garrow

ALL RIGHTS RESERVED
All rights reserved. Without limiting the rights under the copyright reserved above, no part of this publication may be reproduced, stored in, or introduced into a retrieval system, or transmitted in any form or by any means (electronic, mechanical, photocopying, recording, or otherwise) without prior written permission.

ISBN: 9798615723056
Imprint: Independently published

1

Saturday 16th July 1955

Pushing my way through the crowd, I found the exit of the club and banged through the door onto a small landing that led to the steps at the back. The door clattered open again immediately, its handle knocking lumps of plaster off the wall onto a beer-stained linoleum floor. I watched as the couple hurried past me, down the steps and out into the night. Taking a moment to get my breath, I leaned against the rotted wooden banister and half-listened to Ricky's honeyed voice launch into a jazz version of *All of Me*, in time to the regular thumpety-thump of the drums. The music had given me a headache and I wasn't looking forward to my own turn on stage. As it turned out, I wouldn't be doing any singing that night.

Away from the smoky atmosphere of the main hall, the air had a sharpness to it, and the oppressive heat that had engulfed me all evening finally began to lift. A young couple banged in through the outside door at the bottom of the stairs, struggled drunkenly upwards and deposited themselves in front of me, leaning against the telephone on the wall, blocking the landing and my exit.

'Alright, pet?' said the man, swivelling his head towards me. He smirked, then stuck his tongue down the girl's throat, as if this might be the romantic spectacle I'd been waiting for. I resisted rolling my eyes and squeezed past their gyrating hips, shouting apologies above the din. Glancing back at them, the woman's glistening eyes caught mine. With her skirt around her waist and one greasy hand pulling at her suspenders, I could see she thought something magical might be happening. I didn't envy her the prospect.

Outside, I took a few deep breaths, savouring the salty tang in the air. The toilets lay across the lane, and not for the first time, I half-wished I'd been born a man. Other than the stink of piss, the lavatorial structure posed no obstacle for the average Johnny Dangler, but the place threatened an ordeal to be avoided at all costs for anyone in a skirt.

I considered hanging on until one of the other girls came out, then at least we could brave the nightmare together, but my bladder protested.

Crossing the cobbled lane, I gave the left-hand door a shove. It creaked open, revealing only darkness. Digging into my purse, I pulled out the matchbook I'd picked up on the bar. Tearing one off, I stepped into the entrance, shielding the match from the breeze. It ignited first time, illuminating three cubicles. One of the doors hung at an angle, its top hinge shattered. The middle booth stood open but the stench from an overflowing toilet ruled that one out too. The match had almost burned out, so I moved along to the next door and gave it a push. The door bumped against something and creaked shut again. If there'd been anyone in there, they'd have said something, or at least announced their presence. I pushed again, harder this time, and felt a give in the door, as if a sackful of rags had been wedged behind it.

The match went out, causing a yelp to emerge from my throat. Fumbling with the matchbook, lest some ghastly spectre might take the opportunity to drag me down into the depths of Hell, I managed to tear off another match and strike it before my imagination got the better of me. Turning sideways, I squeezed between the damp wall and the edge of the door. Holding the flickering flame in front of myself, I leaned forwards.

And there she was. Half-naked and barefoot, legs stuck at an awkward angle against the back of the door, head resting on the lid of the toilet bowl as if she might be studying the excretions of its last customer. A pool of dark liquid had gathered on the stone floor, the raw, acrid scent filling my nostrils. I had no need to wonder where the blood had come from—the gash in her neck told the story plainly enough.

It was only the act of throwing up that stopped me from screaming.

Four Days Earlier—
Wednesday 13th July 1955

I came home the day they hanged Ruth Ellis.

London to Newcastle on a wet Wednesday isn't a memorable journey at the best of times, and with two deaths in one week, I wasn't looking forward to the consequences in either case. Not that I had anything in common with poor Ruth, but I could sympathise, you know, with the way it had all gone down the pan for her. Another girl looking to carve out a name for herself and ending up with a posh boy who ought to have known better. And any fool could see how it'd play out in the papers—stringing-up a woman had a touch of the barbaric to it and already the 'voices of the people' were calling for changes in the law.

And what did she do, apart from give a bloke what he deserved? In her position, I would have done the same.

'Course, they say Geordie lasses are tougher than average and if a man takes the piss, he's liable to get a rolling pin across the back of his head. But that's one of those pigeonholes, isn't it? Putting folk in boxes where they don't belong. I'd fallen into the same trap myself, 'cos knowing damn well my accent wouldn't do me any favours in London, I'd gone through hell to get rid of it. Now I knew it'd been a waste of time.

But it wasn't Ruth Ellis dangling from a rope that brought me home. It was my mam.

According to our Sheila, the silly cow had tripped on a broken paving stone coming out of the house and stumbled into the road. And you know Campbell Street — a car round there's a rare sight at the best of times, and even on those occasions you'd be hard pushed to hit twenty miles an hour without mowing down the inevitable bunch of kids playing footy along the doors.

Distraction. That's what did it. A furniture salesman in a battered Ford delivery van. Looking at something he shouldn't have been looking at — Ivy Paterson and her fool of a husband bolstering the northern wifie/rolling pin myth right there on their own front doorstep — but it was enough of a diversion to lose concentration. Enough to let the steering wheel slide too far, enough to bounce my mam on the Ford's nearside wing and put her in the RVI. And you know what hospitals are like — only useful if they can fix what's broken. In Mam's case, they couldn't.

Forcing such thoughts to the back of my mind, I ran a comb through my hair and checked my makeup. Definitely not the smiling hopeful I'd been five years back, but it'd do for Tyneside. By the time we passed Sheffield, I had the compartment to myself. Slipping my heels off, I popped my feet up on the seat opposite, tried to catch forty winks. I must've dropped off for the clatter of the door gave me a start.

The temptation to leave my feet where they were didn't get the better of me. Good manners cost nowt, as my mam would say. 'Sorry.' I fumbled my shoes back on and pulled my shoulder bag closer.

The newcomer smelled of Brylcreem and beer, with a hint of something gone-off lurking in the background. My eyes slid up and down as he took off his hat and tossed it onto the luggage rack above my head. He had a film star look about him — slicked-back hair and double-breasted jacket I could believe had come from one of those smart London boutiques, if he hadn't boarded the train at Doncaster. A fancy watch and a gold tiepin suggested a businessman, but I'd seen this type all too often — as soon as he opened his mouth, I'd know for sure.

The compartment had six seats, and of course he plumped for the one across from me. *Fair enough, I'll give him that* — we all like a window seat.

'Going all the way, are you?' And there it was,

the silky-smooth voice, like he's making conversation for the hell of it, but the leering mouth gave him away. If he hoped for a quick one in the lavvy, he'd be out of luck.

'Newcastle.' My attention turned back to the window.

'You finished with that?' He nodded at the newspaper beside me.

'Help yourself.'

'Don't usually read the Mail, of course.' He sniffed and cast an eye over the headline. 'Ah. Miss Ellis. Got what she deserved, then?'

'Depends on your point of view, doesn't it?' I glared at him.

He smirked. 'Female perspective, eh?'

'What's that supposed to mean?'

He blinked. 'You're a woman.'

'And with a knack for observation like that, you must be a copper.'

He laughed, but I could see I'd annoyed him. Leaning forwards, his mouth opened. At the same instant, the door banged open again, and a young couple stumbled in.

'Here we are, luv.' A pasty-faced man about my age heaved two suitcases into the foot space between the seats. Behind him a very pregnant woman with a face that'd seen hard times, forced her way through the door and fell into the nearest pew.

'There ye go, lass.' The man stood over her, grinning. He looked at me, at Mister Brylcreem and observed, 'Newcastle?'

We both nodded, then I went back to gazing out of the window, at the long gardens and allotments flickering past, like one of those old silent movies run at the wrong speed.

Brylcreem regaled the young couple with his opinions about the hanging and even with my head turned away, I could feel him throwing glances at me, trying for a reaction. The newcomers weren't particular in their views on the whole thing and after a few minutes a silence fell over us.

We got into Central Station shortly after two o'clock, and for a change, it wasn't raining. I put my case down and considered lighting a fag. Plenty folk had told me they wouldn't do my throat any good, and even though I'd have killed to have a voice like Marlene Dietrich, waking up with a mouth like an ashtray every morning had finally made my mind up. I glanced at the unopened packet of ciggies and chucked them in a bin. Over the road, I took in the shops, the pubs and the rest of the world going about its business. Somehow, I'd expected everything to be different. But five years down south and the only real difference was me. Picking up my suitcase, I turned left and headed up Westmorland Road. Before facing our Sheila, I needed a drink.

The Fountain stood on the corner of Scotswood Road and Rye Hill. It wasn't the sort of place any woman in her right mind would frequent, but I reckoned I'd be alright as the landlord was an old pal.

Pushing through the double doors, I took a squint into the main bar. Six male heads swivelled round to glare at me.

The man nearest scowled and gave his cap a tug. 'No lasses in here, pet.' A couple of his mates sniggered.

My eyes scanned the otherwise empty room. 'Looking for John.'

The first man took a slurp of his pint and went back to his dominoes, but his partner gave me a nod.

'Puttin another barrel on, pet. Gan on through to the lounge bar. Ah'll tell him you're here.'

I let the door swing back and walked through to the other room.

Brass-topped tables covered most of the floor space, four-legged stools sitting upturned on their tops. Even for a Wednesday, the place was dead. I walked over to the hatch and leaned on the counter. From there I could see through to the bar.

A couple of minutes later, the barman appeared, panting from his exertions.

'Lass lookin for ye, Johnny,' said one of the

domino players.

The barman glanced over at me. He'd lost what little hair he had last time I saw him and had gained a few pounds that wouldn't do him any good in the long run. His face sagged and he tried a smile.

'Rosie. Long-time no see.' He reached up a hand and slid a wine glass off the rack above his head. 'Gin?'

I nodded.

Taking his time, as if seeking to postpone the inevitable, he poured a double, then prising the cap off a bottle of tonic, poured half of it into the glass.

As he walked across to the hatch, I noticed one foot dragged a little and I recalled some story about a local hoodlum with a knife.

'Sorry about yer mam.'

'Yes.'

'Bad business, that.'

I knocked back a mouthful and put the glass back on the counter, gripping the stem too tightly. 'Yes. An accident.'

He pursed his lips and looked away. 'Aye.' Then raising his eyes to mine, shook his head. 'Your Sheila told us. Friday.'

I nodded.

'Me and the wife went up to see her in hospital, but...' He studied the counter, drumming his fingers as if to fill the silence.

'Nother one ower here, John,' called the scowler,

giving me a dirty look. There was something familiar about his face, but I couldn't place it. The voice too, with its harsh cackling laugh, seemed to trigger something in my memory. I pushed it out of my mind. More than likely he reminded me of one of the many weirdos I'd known in London.

'Aye, in a minute.' John half-turned and I could tell he wanted to get on.

I pulled my bag around and began rooting for my purse. 'What do I owe you?'

'Nah, ye're alright, bonny lass.' He sighed and looked at me. 'Ye stayin' wi' your Sheila?'

I let out a sudden laugh. 'She'll not want me up there at her new place. No, I'll stay at Mam's.'

'Well, if you need anything…'

As it happened, there were things I needed, but this wasn't the time, so I fastened up my bag and finished the gin. 'Thanks.'

Outside, the sky had darkened, a storm on the way. Heading around the corner, I continued up to Elswick Road and crossed over into Havelock Street. Without realising it, I counted my steps along to the turning, remembering a game me and my sister used to play — guessing how many steps we'd to take before reaching our front door. Sheila didn't play fair in those days, pushing me out the way so she'd win every time. I'd no reason to think she'd be any different now.

Gazing up at the rows of red-bricked houses, the

place looked the same, but smaller, as if the streets had slid together to keep out the cold. Above me, a line of dull reddish chimneys belched grey smoke into the sky. If I'd wanted a familiar picture to make me feel at home, this was as close as I'd get.

At the door, I pulled out my keys, half-expecting Sheila to have changed the locks. But she hadn't. Turning the knob, I pushed, as someone gave the door a yank.

'Oh. Ye're here, then?' My sister's mouth hadn't lost its lopsided sneer. Jerking her head, she turned and disappeared down the passage.

I followed the back of her head into the front room—a space we'd rarely used growing up and one reserved for people my mam considered important, or those she wanted to keep at a distance. I reckoned Sheila regarded me in the latter category.

The room smelled of lavender and something clinical. I noticed the nets had been washed and several ornaments were missing from their allotted places on the mantelpiece.

'Come up to ours, if you want,' said Sheila, picking a bit of fluff off her cardigan. 'Sure we can find a space for ye somewhere.' She made it sound like this would be a massive inconvenience.

'No, you're alright. My old room'll do fine.'

She looked at me for a moment. 'See ye've lost your accent?'

'Not lost,' I said.

She cleared her throat. 'When ye due back?'

'Want rid of me already?'

She made a sound I supposed she classed as a laugh. 'Course not. Just… Ye know?'

'Is there anything in?' I said, nodding towards the kitchen.

'Milk in the fridge. And bread, but ye'll need to go up to Ahmed's.'

I gave her a look.

'Corner shop.' She sniffed. 'Thought ye'd have loads of them down south.'

'We've got shops right enough. And corners.'

Sheila tried a smile, but it didn't knit with the rest of her face. 'Howay up to ours for tea.' She picked up a lime green jacket that lay over the back of the sofa. 'I'll need to gan an put Bob's tea on, anyway.'

'I had a late lunch,' I said.

'Lunch? We call it dinner round here, ye know?' She coughed and walked to the window, straightening an imaginary crease in the curtains.

'Anyway, I'm tired,' I said. 'Want to get an early night.'

Sheila's face tightened. Crossing to the door, she stopped, our shoulders almost touching. 'Funeral's tomorrah. At St Cuthbert's, then the church hall afterwards.'

'You said on the phone.'

'Right.' Leaning sideways, she gave me what she

probably imagined to be a sisterly hug, patting my arm. 'Ah'm usually at home all day anyway, so…'

'You gave up your job?'

Her mouth twisted. 'Bob didn't want iz workin. An' Ah've plenty to keep me busy, wi' the bairns an' that.'

'I see.' Except, I didn't. Though being a stay-at-home-wife was the done thing in the north east, growing up, we'd always planned to at least try to have careers—even if they turned out to be shitty little jobs in shitty little factories.

In the passage, she turned. 'We can't all go swanning off to London, ye know?'

And there it was—the jealousy, the leave-me-to-deal-with-Mam accusations, the thankless tasks she'd been lumbered with.

'Well, I'm here now.'

'Aye. So ye are.' She paused, one hand on the door. 'Best be up at ours for ten.'

'We're going from yours?'

'Why not?'

This was my sister asserting her authority. She knew tradition decreed the funeral procession leave from the family home. I said, 'Neighbours'll not be happy.'

She snorted. 'Fuck 'em—it's not their funeral.'

Banging the door on her way out, she went off down the street towards the bus stop, glancing back at me through the front window, her face a strange mixture of annoyance and envy.

Walking through into the kitchen, the knot in my stomach tightened and I leaned against the back door, breathing deeply to hold the tears at bay. It wasn't like we'd ever been close. Sheila was the youngest, and the favourite. Somehow, she'd always got what she wanted. And yet I was the one who left home.

2

The front door banged open and running feet clattered up the stairs, a girl's voice shouting, 'Rosie, Rosie, where are ye, man?'

I sat up with a jerk, staring at the bedroom door. But there were no footsteps, no nine-year-old Sheila yelling for me to *howay-down-the-street-and-see*. A dream, then, or another bad memory. The room seemed bright. I'd forgotten how pathetic the curtains were—light streaming through as if they weren't there. Pulling the blankets back, I rolled out of bed, forgetting it was higher than my double divan back in Soho's Greek Street. Mind you, neither the bed nor the street were anything to brag about.

I sorted out my clothes for the funeral and had a bath. By the time I'd got ready, I still had an hour to kill, so I made another cup of coffee then went out to get the bus up to Sheila's.

Bob and Sheila lived in a nineteen-thirties-built semi off West Road, near the cricket ground. Nicer than Mam's house for sure, but I'd always thought the area had an atmosphere about it, as if the residents believed themselves to be better than their council-house counterparts.

Sheila's eldest opened the door, face smeared with chocolate, one hand fiddling with his crotch.

'Me mam sez you're a minger.' He grinned up at me, then turned and bounced his way down the passage as Sheila emerged from a room on the right.

'Ah said she's a *singer*, ye little shit.' She pulled the door wide, and waved me in. 'Sorry pet. Ten years old, an' he's a bleedin' liability already.' Her face had gone a nice shade of pink, though whether from genuine embarrassment, or hearing her offspring repeat one of her own offhand remarks, I couldn't tell.

She waved me into the house, and I followed the sound of the devil-boy's laughter into the back room. Kneeling on the floor in the middle of the room, best suit trousers rolled up to the knees, Sheila's husband wrestled with the buttons on his youngest's blouse.

'Now leave it alone, will ye?' He gave the girl a playful smack, hauled himself up into a standing position and did a little dance to shake his trouser legs back to their usual position. 'Aye-aye, Rosie.'

I allowed myself to fall into an awkward embrace, his clumsy hands pawing at my body as if he'd never encountered a real woman before.

Stepping back, I folded my arms in a bid to stave off any further contact. 'Good to see you, Bob.

You're looking well.'

'Aye.' He gave a shrug, his eyes scanning my chest. 'Ye look canny in black.'

'Thanks.' I looked around, keen for some diversion. 'My, haven't you shot up?'

The girl dropped her chin, eyeing me coyly. Turning to her father, she whispered, 'Who is it?'

Bob laughed a little too enthusiastically. 'This is your Auntie Rosie. Remember what we told ye?'

The girl looked up at me again. 'Are you a singer?'

'I am.'

'Are ye to sing a song, then?'

Bob gave her a gentle push. 'Don't be cheeky, Dora, your Auntie's come for the funeral.' He glanced at the clock on the mantle. 'They'll be here shortly.'

'How many cars are there for the family?' I said.

'Erm…' He looked past me. 'Sheila?'

My sister appeared at my elbow like a pantomime genie doing her three-wishes routine. 'Just the one.' She cocked her head to one side. 'Well, not as if Aunt Vera an' them gave a flying fuck about her, was it?'

Bob exhaled noisily. 'Sheila, man, not in front of the bloody bairns.'

My sister glanced at Dora, who smiled up at her as if to say, "Bad Mammy".

Dropping her voice to barely a hiss, Sheila

prodded her husband's chest with an angry finger, emphasising her words. 'Just lost me mam, have Ah not? Am'nt Ah entitled to swear if Ah need ter?' She turned and stormed off up the stairs.

Bob coughed. 'She's a bit on edge.'

'Maybe you should let her go back to work, Bob?' I said, trying to keep any hint of accusation out of my voice.

His hands dropped to his sides. 'Ah wish she bloody would, pet, but she'll not be telt. The bairns need her here, she says. Housework'd never get done, she says. Ah've said time an' again, it'd be good for her to get out the house, but she'll not be on, man.'

Having believed Sheila's explanation, it occurred to me there might be another reason why she wanted to stay indoors. But I said nothing.

When the cars arrived, we all trooped out of the house under the watchful gaze of the local community. I recognised a few faces, friends of Sheila and Bob's, but otherwise they were strangers, no doubt keen to stay abreast of current events. A group of sombre-looking individuals had gathered near the house. I spotted a cluster of distant cousins and a great-aunt who'd brought us toys a couple of times at Christmas. I couldn't recall anything about her other than she'd had a pretty impressive chin growth that had amused Sheila and I no end.

I sat on one of the fold-down seats opposite Dora and the devil-boy. Bob kept one hand on his son's arm, ensuring the lad remained seated. Behind us, a few cars pulled out and attached themselves to the procession.

As we approached the church, I spied Aunt Vera and Uncle Maurice standing at the gates like statues, faces impassive and granite-like. A group of distant relatives gathered behind them, all in black and all sporting similarly expressionless gazes.

Our car followed the hearse as it nosed in through the gates, forcing the group to back away. Pulling up at the church door, we watched for a moment, as the funeral director and his crew made preparations to carry the coffin into the church.

Dora and Devil-Boy had fallen quiet and I felt a sudden surge of emotion when I saw a tear run down Dora's little face, her lower lip quivering.

'Come on, then,' said Bob, pushing open the car door. 'Let's get it over with.'

I don't recall much of the service, expect that we sang Mam's favourite hymn, *Abide with Me*, provoking streams of tears from myself and my sister. After that, we somehow arrived at the graveside where the vicar prattled on about what a good neighbour Mam had been and how she'd be missed in the community. Considering she hadn't been inside a church in twenty-odd years, and had likely never met him, I guessed these were stock phrases rattled out like run-of-the-mill platitudes at such occasions.

As the mourners wandered off, I hung back. Vera and Maurice came over and I gave them both a hug, while they muttered the usual clichés. I wondered if they'd been making notes during the service.

'Ye'll be heading back down south, then?' said Maurice, rubbing a hand down my arm as if I were a pet dog.

'That's the plan.'

'Spect it's all go, down there, eh?' This from Vera, whose features held onto their flinty countenance. Her resentment at being excluded from the 'family' car was obvious.

'It's a bit different to Newcastle,' I said, delivering one of my own stock phrases.

Maurice chuntered on about how his kid sister had been a bit of tomboy in her youth, while Vera chipped in with occasional criticisms on the folly of marrying young. But something else had caught my attention—hovering near the church and glancing my way, John from the Fountain gave me a nod. Excusing myself, I walked over and shook his hand.

'Thanks for coming.'

'Aye. Wanted to say goodbye to her, ye know?'

We both studied the grass and I noticed he wore the same battered shoes he'd had on in the bar. I guessed this was his only suit, too.

'Actually,' he peered over my shoulder, then putting a hand on my elbow, led me to one side. 'Ah wanted a word.'

'About Mam?'

'What? No, lass. No.' He chewed his lip for a moment, then, 'It's Ricky.'

The knot in my stomach came back with a vengeance and I felt more than a pang of annoyance at John for having brought the subject up.

'What's he want?'

John laughed. 'Ye know what he wants, bonny lass.'

Half-turning, I glanced over at Aunt Vera. She'd collared Bob and seemed to be giving him a good talking to.

'I've moved on.'

He smiled. 'That's what Ah told him, but Ah don't think it's only about the music.'

'Then what?'

His eyes swerved to one side. 'Why don't ye ask him.'

Turning, I saw a lone figure standing by the gates, hands in pockets, eyes gazing at everyone but me, as if unwilling to acknowledge my existence.

'Fuck's sake.' Waiting until he looked straight at me, I raised an eyebrow and stared at him. I saw the sigh, the realisation that I wasn't going to walk over there. He stomped across, weaving between gravestones, trying to look cool.

He'd filled out a bit since I last saw him and his face had a more chiselled look than I remembered. The hairstyle was new.

'Tryin to look like Dean Martin?'

He twitched and slid a hand through his hair. 'Nah. Part of the act, that's all.'

'Still got the band, then?'

'Aye. Doin' alright, actually.' Dropping his head, he leaned closer. 'Sorry about yer mam.'

'Thanks.'

He seemed about to say something, then turned and gazed over at Aunt Vera. 'Your Sheila still not talking to her?'

I looked at my auntie, searching her stony features for some sign of why this might be. Sheila, meanwhile, had placed herself a good twenty yards away, with her back to Vera. Knowing Sheila had never liked our mother's sister, I guessed any falling-out between them would have something to do with the funeral arrangements. 'No, apparently not.'

Ricky started whistling some tuneless melody in what I took to be his version of nonchalance. 'So ye'll be going back shortly, eh?'

'Why does everybody want to know when I'm leaving?'

He shrugged. 'Just…ye know…if ye were goin' to be around for a bit, like…'

'Join the band again?' I laughed. 'Julie needs a backing singer, does she?'

His face creased up and I sensed I'd hit a nerve.

'Julie's alright, isn't she?' My best pal in the old days had taken over the role of singer when I headed for the bright lights of London.

'She's left us.'

'Left you, or left the band?'

'Both, Ah suppose.'

'Rick...' I struggled for something that'd sound reasonable. 'There's no point me getting involved again, not just for a few days.'

'Ye could do a guest spot.'

'What? Famous singer returns to her native northeast?' I shook my head. 'Don't think so. Even if I *was* famous.'

'Folk remember ye, though. An' it's at the Majestic.'

'Really?' I didn't expect this — the Majestic wasn't some smoky dive in the backstreets of Newcastle, but a venue frequented by some of the north east's top bands.

'Going up in the world, are you?'

'Come on, Rosie, ye'd be doin' us a big favour...'

I knew damn well it wasn't about helping out my old band, but I couldn't see Ricky telling me the truth, whatever it might be. 'Saturday?'

'Aye. We can pay ye, an'all.'

'Wow, money too?'

'Divvent tek the piss.' He smiled and for a moment I saw him as he'd looked back then, the two of us inseparable, always giggling, happy.

'Fine.'

'Ye stayin' at yer mam's?'

I nodded.

'Ah could pop in tomorrah. Go over a few songs, an that.'

We agreed a time and I watched him walk away towards the gates. John hovered further along the path, making a big show of reading a dedication on one of the older gravestones. Seeing me watching, he gave me a dopey grin and came over.

'He talked ye round, eh?'

'What do you think?'

'Aye.' He sniffed. 'Shame about Julie, like.'

'Music was always more important to Ricky than women. Serves him right if she went off with someone else.'

He gazed off into the distance. 'If she did.'

'How'd you mean?'

He let out a long sigh. 'Oh, nowt. Just…' He dug his hands into his pockets, mouth twisting as if unable to get the words out.

'Come on, then. What?'

'He *says* she was always on about leavin', an' that, but to vanish…'

It wasn't like John to be cagey, but I had to coax it out of him, bit by bit. It seemed Julie had gone to make a phone call one night after a gig and had never come back. Her and Ricky had argued about something and he'd convinced himself some mysterious admirer had whisked her off somewhere, never to return. But that didn't sound like the Julie I knew.

'When was this?'

He shook his head. 'Coupla weeks, maybe three.'

I saw our Sheila making her way down the path towards me. 'You coming over to the hall, John?'

'Got to get back, but Ah'll have a cup of tea.'

The rest of the day slid by in a blur, with distant aunts and cousins offering their condolences and the occasional anecdote about Mam. Half the faces meant nothing to me and those I did remember weren't people I particularly wanted to see.

At four o'clock, Bob began making let's-go-home noises and the stragglers said their goodbyes. By six o'clock I was back at Mam's and too tired to do anything else.

Something woke me up and it took me a moment to get my head around the fact that I was lying in my old bed in Mam's house in Newcastle. Then I recalled the dream, but I must've jolted myself awake before it got going. I lay still, gazing up at the ceiling for ages, before summoning up the motivation to drag myself out of bed.

Ricky turned up in time for coffee. He'd brought his old Fender acoustic along but didn't seem keen to do anything with it.

'Two sugars, still?'

'Aye.'

I'd taken him into the back room, which at least felt normal. Leaning his guitar case against the sideboard, he walked over and sat in my dad's old chair by the hearth. For a moment I had the urge to tell him to move, but it'd only make him more uncomfortable than he already was, so I kept quiet.

I pushed the plate of biscuits across the coffee table.

'Ta.' Balancing his cup on the arm of the chair, he shuffled forwards and reached for the plate. 'Custard creams. Me favourites.'

'Got them specially,' I said, thankful Mam always kept a stock of them in the top cupboard, in case her girls ever bothered to come round for tea.

'So. What about this gig?'

'We're on at eight. Forty-five minutes, then a break, then we'll get you on.' He cocked his head to one side. 'If that's okay?'

'I'll do three songs. That's all.'

He bit his lip. 'Great.'

'Stormy Weather…'

'Good choice.'

'Love for Sale?'

He nodded. 'Sure, though I'll need to check the

chords.'

'And maybe a bit of Hank Williams—Your Cheatin Heart?'

He smiled. 'Be just like old times, eh?'

'Almost.'

We chatted about music for a while, then Ricky drained his cup and pushed it back onto the table. 'So we'll pick you up about four.'

'Pick me up? You got transport?'

He flushed. 'Joe has a van. Makes things a lot easier.'

I smiled, remembering how we used to drag all the gear onto the bus whenever we had a gig.

'An' we'll drop you home after.'

'I should hope so.'

He looked like he wanted to say something else. In fact, he'd looked that way all morning. I realised it wasn't fair to make him do all the work.

'What happened with Julie?'

His shoulders sagged and he seemed to relax, as if I'd removed an obstacle.

'She didn't just leave,' he said. A long pause, then, 'See, she told iz she had ter make a phone call…'

'John said. He also said you'd argued.'

Ricky rolled his eyes. 'Hardly an argument. She wasn't happy about a couple of gigs Ah'd lined up.'

'You think she went off with someone?'

Closing his eyes, he shook his head. 'Wish Ah

knew.' Leaning forwards, he got all animated. 'No-one's seen her, not her mam, her brother, nobody. It's like she vanished.'

'Did you report it to the cops?'

He nodded. 'Yeah, well, her mam did. But they said she's an adult. Took her purse and keys with her, so…'

I thought about Ruth Ellis. 'You think something bad's happened?'

'Oh, Christ, Ah don't know, do Ah?'

'She was always a bit flighty,' I said.

'Ah know, but…'

We talked some more about the old days, but I didn't want to go too far down that road. Not just yet, anyway.

Climbing into the battered old van, I slid behind the driver's seat onto a packing case strapped to the wall.

'Here she is, man,' said Joe, leaning over to give me a kiss. 'Wor very own somebody.'

In the front sat Ricky and a younger man, who I guessed would be the bass player. In a suede green jacket and a bright orange shirt, I could see the current fashion trends hadn't curbed his imagination.

'Hi. You must be Mick.'

'Sure. Heard lots about ye, pet.' He gave Ricky a dig with an elbow. 'Lots.'

I glanced at Ricky. 'I bet you have.'

By the time we'd set up and run through my songs a few times, it had gone six. Ricky had treated himself to a second-hand Gibson Les Paul and wanted to try it out. He played a couple of solos and I had to admit to feeling a little taken aback at how much his technique had improved since the last time I'd seen him perform.

The doors opened at seven, and the place wouldn't liven up until at least eight o'clock, so we had time to kill. Joe and Mick jammed open the stage door to have a few smokes — the place'd be smoky enough later on. I retreated to the dressing room, such as it was, and slipped into the one posh frock I'd brought with me. I wasn't due on stage until after nine, so I made my way back down to the main bar in search of refreshment.

My heels clip-clopped across the floor, echoing around the room and announcing my approach to the only other person in the hall. The dark-haired guy behind the bar watched me, polishing shot-glasses as if he had better things to do. Like Ricky, he had the Dean Martin haircut and looked as if he'd been practising the sultry-eyed stares to go with it.

He gave me a friendly nod. 'You part of the band, are ye?'

'Tonight I am, yes.'

'Better get ye a drink, then. What ye havin?'

'Haven't made up my mind, yet.'

He peered at me. 'Ah know you, don't Ah?'

'Dunno. Do you?'

His mouth fell open. 'Course. It's little Rosie isn't it? Aye.' He nodded. 'Westgate Primary.'

'You *are* joking?'

'Course, yer hair was proper red in those days.' He laughed, as if he'd caught me in an awkward situation.

Staring at him now, there did seem to be something familiar about his face, and particularly that wonky nose. 'Oh God. Eddie Reid.' My hand flew to my mouth, the memory of what I'd done at the forefront of my mind.

'Pushed me off the fucking wall, didn't yer? Never been the same since.' He pointed to his nose and laughed.

'I *was* only six…'

'Aye, right enough. Still…'

We both smiled and an uneasy silence dropped over us. He resumed polishing the glasses.

'Used to sing down at The Bridge a while back.'

I shrugged. 'Few years ago.'

'Ah heard ye'd gone to London.'

'That's right.'

'And now ye're back?'

'Well…'

'Rick'll be chuffed, eh?'

'I'm not back. Not exactly.'

He moved along the bar, sliding glasses into the allotted places on the shelves. I picked up a matchbook from the ashtray, turning it round in my fingers. It had the Majestic's name printed on the front in black and red lettering, and the club's phone number on the back.

'Did you know Julie?'

He half turned. 'Who?'

'Julie. She sang with Ricky and them before.'

He stopped and leaned across the bar. Dropping his voice, he said, 'She's the one that went missin.'

'You heard about that?'

'Aye. Cops were in, asking questions.'

'What? She went missing from here?' Ricky hadn't mentioned this, and I felt my stomach give a jolt.

He sniffed. 'Divvent think they did much, mind. Not like she got murdered or owt.'

The possibility that something bad had happened to Julie crossed my mind but hearing him say it out loud, even if he didn't believe it, made it feel real.

Two hands grabbed me from behind. 'Better get backstage, pet.'

'Jezaz, Ricky! Ah nearly shit meself.'

'Nearly lost your posh accent an'all,' he said, sniggering at Eddie, as if sharing a dirty joke.

I pushed him away and turned back to the barman. 'Can I get a cup of tea, Eddie?'

'Anythin for you, pet,' he murmured, glancing at Ricky. 'Kettle's round the back. Give iz a minute.' He disappeared through a door at the side.

'Didn't know you two knew each other?'

'Well, it appears you don't know everything about me, doesn't it, Richard.'

'Ye'll be shaggin him, next.'

My hand was out before I could stop it, catching him right across the face. 'What the fuck's that supposed to mean?'

'God, Rosie, Ah was only havin a laugh.' He rubbed his injured face and I felt myself redden.

'Sorry.' I reached up and kissed his cheek. 'Won't do it again.'

He swivelled away from me and leaned an elbow on the bar.

'Ricky?'

'What?'

'I'm sorry, it's just…'

He peered at me over his shoulder. Raised an eyebrow.

'Well, it's just that it's been a while since…'

He coughed and turned to face me. 'Yeah, well.'

We agreed to let it go and waited in silence until Eddie brought my tea, then I followed Ricky into the dressing room where Joe and Mick were doing a rude version of *My Old Man*, Joe tapping on the back of a chair with his drumsticks and Mick thumbing his double bass in the corner.

I'd intended staying off any alcohol until after my spot, but Joe produced a crate of stout — part of the band's fee, apparently — and we didn't want it going to waste, did we? Before the first set, I shared a bottle with Ricky and thinking it'd help me relax a bit, opened another one for myself. Picking up his acoustic, Ricky strummed through my first number, but I could barely manage to get out a single note, the butterflies in my stomach well into their stride. It was always the same before I went on stage — I knew it'd be fine once I was up there and we got going, but until we did, I always felt a bit crap.

Once the doors opened, the space filled up — couples and groups of threes and fours surging in to grab a good spot at one of the tables around the outskirts of the room. Others swarmed straight to the front, leaning their elbows on the stage to stake their places while their mates got the drinks in. I found myself relegated to a spot at the side of the stage where I could watch the lads go through the first set. The crowd were a good-natured lot, though I knew from experience at least of couple of fights would break out later. As usual, it took a few songs to get the audience going, to loosen up and allow themselves to enjoy the music.

It felt good to hear some of the old songs again, though I did think the lads could've done with updating their material. More punters poured in during the first set and I remember feeling glad I'd stood near the fire escape — if there happened to be an emergency, it'd be chaos trying to get everyone out at once.

Someone nudged my elbow and I turned around.

'Aye, aye.'

'Aye, aye, yourself,' I said.

I guessed he must've been a good fifteen years younger than me, with a suit probably borrowed off his dad. His face bore the evidence of someone not used to shaving, but he had a nice smile.

'Rosie, isn't it?'

'What if it is?'

'Used ter see yer doon at the Bridge. Few years back.'

'Can't be that many years back — looks like you've only been out of school a month.' I grinned, playfully.

'Oh aye, very funny, like. No, but Ah did see yous a few times.' He took a slurp from his pint. 'Great voice.'

'Then let's hope I've still got it.'

'Buy ye a drink if ye like?'

Slipping into my native twang, I said, 'Ah think ye're a bit young for me, bonny lad. Gan on an find yersel a younger model.'

He laughed. 'Oh, whey man, canna blame a lad for tryin.' He gave me a wink and wandered back to his mates.

The lads ended their set with *Cotton Crop Blues*, a James Cotton song that had an authentic American blues feel to it and allowed Ricky to show off his soloing prowess on the Gibson. It went down a storm with the crowd and lots of couples were up on the floor dancing.

Back in the dressing room, I'd begun to feel a bit woozy, and knocked back a glass of cold water to clear my head.

Ricky bounced around the room, full of energy. Thumping himself down next to me, he slid a hand along the back of the sofa. I gave him a hard stare and he made an *'Oops, sorry'* face.

'Remind me — when am I on?'

Pulling a slip of paper from his pocket, he ran a finger down the set list. 'We're on again at nine. We'll do *All of Me* and T-Bone Walker's *Bobby Sox Blues*, then I'll introduce you.' He patted my leg. 'You'll be great. Ah'll do the whole big-star-from-the-big-city thing. Get them going a bit.'

'Whatever you think's best.'

Fifteen minutes later, they were back on stage and I found my space between the side door and the speakers for the PA system.

Perhaps due to standing too close to the speakers, my head started to thump, and I wished I'd stuck to my principles and stayed off the beer. But it was too late now. Scanning the crowd for friendly faces — folk like Eddie who I might've gone to school with, or had known from the pub circuit we'd been used to before the clubs opened up to our particular brand of entertainment—I noticed how youthful the audience were compared to myself and the band, and suddenly felt really old. Remembering my first thought on stepping off the train from London, I realised it wasn't only me who'd changed.

The effects of the beer and the rising heat in the room persuaded me to nip to the toilets, otherwise I'd be concentrating on not wetting my knickers instead of putting on a good show.

Pushing my way through the crowd, I found the exit of the club and banged through the door onto a small landing that led to the steps at the back. The door clattered open again immediately, its handle knocking lumps of plaster off the wall onto a beer-stained linoleum floor. I watched as the couple hurried past me, down the steps and out into the night. Taking a moment to get my breath, I leaned against the rotted wooden banister…

3

It wasn't Julie.

Eddie's revelation that she'd gone missing had been running around in the back of my mind all night and before I even opened the toilet door and saw her face, the thought that it might be her, had hit me like a sack of coal.

But this girl was too tall, and the blood splashed across her young face did nothing to hide the shock in her dull grey eyes.

I don't remember how I got back up the stairs into the club, but I ended up at one end of the bar, clinging to the brass rail and gaping at Eddie. He must've seen something in my face for he was at my side in an instant, holding me up, half carrying me through the peering faces towards the dressing room. Swinging my head around, I looked at him, saw his lips moving but no sound reached my ears. Then Ricky's voice boomed over the PA system, saying something about me coming all the way from the bright lights of London. Then he stopped talking and it seemed as if the whole place fell silent, all eyes on me.

Eddie guided me down the side of the stage and

through into the dressing room, letting me slide down onto the old sofa along the back wall.

'What's happened, pet?'

I looked up at him, struggling to focus my eyes. 'What?'

'Ye look like shit, man. What's happened?'

I blurted it all out, the whole thing, a jumble of words and tears, my hands grasping at him as if I might fall.

'Jezaz wept.' He pressed my shoulders, pushing me back onto the sofa. 'Stay there. Ah'll call the cops.'

Yanking the door open, he collided with Ricky.

'What's gannin on, like?' his voice accusing, argumentative. Then he saw my face and something must've clicked in his brain. 'Oh, Christ, Rosie…'

Down on his knees, his arms engulfed me, pulling me to him.

'She's dead, Ricky.'

'Who's dead?'

My head was shaking, side to side, as if of its own accord.

The man in the raincoat finally stopped talking to someone outside the door and sat down beside me. I turned to look at him.

'Miss Robson, is it?'

I nodded.

'Ah'm Inspector Walton. Are ye up to answering

a few questions?'

I nodded again. He looked young, or at least, younger than you'd expect a Detective Inspector to be. There were a few grey hairs playing around his sideburns, but I guessed he couldn't be more than late thirties.

Taking out a black notebook, he licked the end of his pencil. 'Contact details?'

I told him Mam didn't have a phone and rooted around in my handbag for my little telephone book. 'I can give you my sister's number.'

He made a note of it. 'Ye live with yer mam?'

'No.'

'But this is her address?'

Closing my eyes, I waited for Ricky to fill in the details. He did.

'Ah. Sorry for your loss, pet.' He paused, then, 'And your age?'

I thought about knocking off a couple of years, but that would've been pointless, so I just told him. 'Thirty-four, last month.'

'Good. Now then, from the beginning, please.'

Recounting everything from going down the steps to coming back into the club, I stopped every so often to give him time to make notes. He nodded a few times, made more notes, nodded some more.

'And you were meant to be singing with the band, were ye?'

'Yes.'

'That a regular thing, is it?'

I looked at him. 'How d'you mean?'

He supressed a sigh, smiled. 'Ah mean, you've appeared here before? With the same band?'

'No. That is, I've played with the band before but not for years. I've been in London, see?'

'And the woman in the…er…toilets. You knew her?'

'No. Don't think so.'

And so it went on. I imagined cops swarming all over the club, blocking off all access to the murder scene, taking names, checking identities.

The door opened and a young copper leaned in. 'The doctor's here, sir.'

The inspector sniffed. He put a hand on my arm. 'We'll need to see you again, but are you alright to go home just now?'

'Ah'll take her home.'

I looked up, having forgotten Ricky was still there, sitting on the dressing table, watching.

The inspector flipped back a few pages in his notepad. 'Richard Dickie?'

'Ricky.'

'Ricky Dickie.' A smile slid across his face. 'And you were on stage at the time Miss Robson discovered the….er…?'

'Aye. I mean, yes, I was.'

The inspector seemed satisfied. Standing, he patted my shoulder. 'Ye've had a shock. Ah suggest you go home, have a cup of sweet tea and get yerself away to bed. Try not to let it play on your mind.'

'Easy for him to say,' I muttered after he'd gone.

'You okay?' Ricky knelt in front of me, his face a picture of concern.

'Have to be, won't I?'

'Ah called your Sheila.'

'Oh, shite. What for?'

'Ah don't think ye should be on your own. Ah said Ah'd take ye up to hers.'

'Thanks a bunch, Rick.' I glanced at my watch. 'It's gone twelve. Bet she was dead chuffed.'

He smiled. 'Ah told her what'd happened an' that.' He took hold of my hand. 'She's concerned for ye.'

Ricky and the lads got their things together and loaded the van. I stood at the end of the bar, gazing at the empty room. I wasn't sure when everyone had gone home, but midnight was early for a place like the Majestic.

'Bit of a downer, eh?'

I looked up. Eddie jerked his head towards the till. 'Buggered up the takings nicely, that did.'

'I'm sure that lassie's really sorry for getting herself killed.'

'Ah didn't mean...' He shook his head. 'Aye, ye're right. More important stuff than money.' Footsteps behind us prompted Eddie to straighten up sharply. Dropping his voice, he murmured, 'Watch out. Frankie Fenwick's comin.'

A tall man approached us. He had a bald head and a puckered mouth like a cat's arse. Standing too close, he glared at me. 'You're the one, then, eh?'

'The one what?'

'Had to close up two hours early, thanks very much.' He glanced at Eddie. 'Ye still here, lad? Time ye fucked off home like the rest of them. Not paying ye for standin round doin' fuck all.'

'Sorry, Frankie. Ah mean, Mr Fenwick. Ah'm just off.' Eddie gave me a surreptitious wink and left.

'So.' The bald man studied me, as if I were an interesting specimen presented for his own private examination. 'Rosie Robson. Didn't expect to see you round here again.'

'I didn't realise we'd met.'

His thin lips curled into a sneer. 'We haven't. But Ah've seen ye before. Down at The Bridge. Good few years back, mind.' He slipped a hand into his waistcoat pocket and pulled out a small white card. 'Fenwick's the name. Might be able to put some work your way.' His tongue slid out and ran along his lower lip. 'If you're willing, that is?'

I didn't want to ask what he thought I might be willing for, though I felt sure it wasn't anything I'd enjoy.

'Not going to be staying round here.' He said nothing so I added, 'Heading back to London, shortly.'

'London. Tch. Well, Ah'll tell yer, they've got nowt down there that we haven't got up here.'

I held out the card to give back to him.

'Keep it. Ye might change your mind. See ye round, pet.' He turned and strode across the hall towards the main entrance.

Ricky appeared at my elbow.

'Who's he — king of the world?'

Ricky watched as the bald man disappeared through the double doors. 'Festering Frankie.' He shrugged. 'He's the owner, though Ah've never had a conversation with him. Doesn't mix with the plebs.' He took my arm. 'Ready?'

He led me down to the stage door and out to the van.

Pulling up outside Sheila's, I felt an unexpected sense of relief to see her standing in the doorway, a housecoat pulled around herself to hide her nightie.

Ricky walked me up the path. 'Ah'll pop over tomorrah, alright?'

'Come on, pet,' said Sheila, taking my arm. 'Thanks Ricky.' She gave him what I can only describe as a normal smile and we stood and watched as he jumped back into the van and sped off up the road.

'Ah've heated up some milk. Hot chocolate.'

As soon as she closed the front door, I collapsed

against her, head on her shoulder, sobbing for all I was worth.

'Bloody hell, pet. What've ye got yersel into this time?' This with her usual dollop of disdain. But she hugged me nevertheless and for the first time in years, I forgot I was meant to be the mature one and slid all too easily into the role of little sister.

She sat me on the living room sofa, laying a blanket over my legs. Bustling into the kitchen she was back in a flash bearing a tray with steaming mugs and chocolate biscuits. Pulling up a side table, she turned the tray around so I wouldn't have to lean forward. Then, as if concerned I might collapse into tears again, carefully eased herself down next to me.

Cupping the mug, I sipped my drink, surprised to find it tasted just like Mam's. It wasn't like Sheila to copy anything Mam did, but this brought back memories I thought I'd forgotten. It almost felt as if she'd accidently turned into Mam. Any other time, this idea would have had me chortling with glee, but now it simply felt normal. Maybe all she'd wanted was to feel needed.

It didn't last.

'So how'd ye get yerself mixed up with a dead woman?'

'I'm not mixed up with her. I found her, that's all.'

'In the toilets, Ricky said.'

'Her throat had been cut.'

'Oh, Jezaz wept…'

'I'd rather not talk about it, if you don't mind?'

She patted my lag. 'No, course not, pet.' She stayed silent for a few minutes, then, 'Would ye like iz to stay up with ye?'

I shook my head. 'No.'

She sniffed and stood. 'Ah've put you in Dora's room. She's in with us.'

'Thanks.'

She patted my leg again and went off upstairs.

Listening to the creaking floorboards above me and Sheila's soothing tones as she settled her child down and told her husband to shut his face, gave me an oddly warm feeling inside. Maybe I'd misjudged my sister, seeing her only from the point of view of an out-of-favour child who had always been at the bottom of the pile.

I chewed through a couple of biscuits, finished the hot chocolate and made my way up to the box room at the back of the house. The blankets had been folded back and a bedside lamp gave the room a radiance my bedroom back at Mam's had never had. Maybe this is what family life was like.

Waking up in a strange bed for the second time that week, gave me a sudden jolt until I remembered where I was. Sounds of cooking and childish arguments drifted up from downstairs.

Sitting up, I noticed the open bedroom door and wondered if Sheila had checked on me during the night. More likely it'd been kids having a nosy.

Rolling out of bed, I crossed the small room and pushed the door to, then opened the curtains and climbed back under the covers. I'd expected to be on my way back to London by now, leaving Sheila to sort out the sale of the house and everything else. Thinking about it, maybe that's what I'd always done—put her and her life into a box labelled *Sheila's Stuff* and used it to justify why I rarely bothered to come home. Now, it seemed, as Sheila had always said, I was the one to blame for her lousy attitude.

Then again, maybe I could put it down to the trauma of finding a corpse. After all, a shock like that—seeing someone's throat sliced open—could turn anybody daft in the head. I probably needed time to come to terms with it. Maybe that police inspector would suggest something. Some sort of counsellor, or therapist like those big Hollywood movie stars had.

The smell of bacon became too much to resist and pulling on my posh frock, I nipped to the bathroom and made myself decent before going down to breakfast.

'Here she is,' said Bob, pulling out a chair at the dining table. He gave me a wide grin, though I saw the questions pasted across his face. What new catastrophes would this has-been singer bring into his household today?

'We saw ye when you was asleep,' said Dora, glancing at her mother.

'Just went in to check, that's all,' said Sheila. She paused, then, 'How ye doin'?'

'Been better.'

'You two nearly finished?' she said to the kids.

Devil-Boy stabbed sausages with his fork and stuffed them into his mouth. 'Yesh.'

'Ah'm not finished, Mam,' said Dora, though her plate looked as if she'd licked it clean.

'Go out an' play, then, eh?'

Dora frowned at her mother, then turned to me. 'Ah'll just stay here.'

'Go out and play, Dora. Now.' This from Bob, though his face told me he'd love to be the one allowed out into the garden, instead of staying in here with the weird sisters.

After another round of grumbling, the siblings departed.

Picking two rashers of bacon off the serving dish (surely reserved for special guests) I buttered toast and waited for the interrogation.

'It's a murder, then, is it?' said Bob.

'I'd say so,' I said, avoiding his eyes. 'The inspector didn't let me in on his theories.'

'But ye'll have to see them again? The police?'

'They want a written statement.'

Bob made a face. 'Wanna be careful what ye put your name to. Wouldn't be the first time the cops dropped some poor fucker in the crap. It's not like *Dixon of Dock Green*, ye know?'

He was referring to a new TV series that had started the week before. I'd quite enjoyed the first episode, but I knew what he meant—real coppers weren't like that.

Bob was into his stride. 'They're not goin' to tap ye on the back of your head and say, run along pet and don't do it again…'

I gave Sheila a pleading look, willing her to make him shut up.

'Ah think me sister knows the difference between fact and fiction, Bob.'

I mouthed a silent thank you. 'By the way, I had to give them your phone number.'

Bob sighed, like this was the last straw. 'Excellent. Ah'll be waiting for their call.' He'd clearly taken over his wife's role as Sarcasm Supremo.

'Well, I don't have a phone, do I?' I said.

He turned to Sheila. 'Didn't yer mam have a phone?'

'Aye, me mam got the phone put in just after she won the Football Pools.' She glared at him. 'Christ, it's like living with a side of beef.'

He couldn't dispute this.

'Speaking of which,' she went on, 'Mam's

house'll be going on sale this week. Tomorrow.' She gave me a pleading look. 'So if you're planning to stay around...'

Bob pushed his plate away, shoved his chair back and walked off.

'I don't think your husband wants me staying here,' I said.

'Oh, fuck him.'

We looked at each other for a long moment, then broke into giggles.

'Serves him right,' she said. 'He's had his own way for too long.'

I folded a slice of toast round two rashers of bacon and started munching. Outside, Dora and Devil-Boy stared in through the window, pressing their faces against the glass and blowing out their cheeks.

Sheila waved them away. 'I suppose ye can stay at Mam's 'til it's sold. Not likely to happen any time soon.' She placed her knife and fork carefully on her plate. 'But ye *are* goin' back?' I couldn't tell from her tone if she wanted rid of me, or if her attitude had undergone some sort of metamorphosis in the last few days.

Leaning forwards, I plonked my elbows on the table and propped my head between my hands. Truthfully, there wasn't that much to go back for, but I'd convinced myself that coming home would be nothing more than a final parting of the ways, a closing of all those little drawers I'd used to file away the past over the years. Now, I wondered if it might be time to pull out all that stuff and lay it to rest properly.

But that was one big cabinet full of shite. And I wasn't sure I'd be up to dealing with it.

I took a breath. 'Jury's still out on that one.'

An hour later, I'd set off walking back to Mam's. Ricky had said he'd come round, though hadn't said when. It wasn't that I particularly wanted to see him again, but at least he'd been there when I needed him and knew what I'd gone through.

I hadn't walked far when I realised high heels weren't the ideal choice for doing the old Shanks' Pony down West Road on a Sunday, with only a posh frock and a skimpy jacket to keep me warm. Unlike some parts of the country, summer in Geordieland didn't necessarily mean good weather. Sitting on a nearby wall to give my feet a rest, I rooted through my handbag in the hope of discovering a forgotten packet of cigarettes, but all I had was those matches. Flipping them open, I saw something I hadn't noticed before. Someone had scribbled a phone number in faded pencil. Squinting at it, the writing had faded but I could just about make it out. It said, *22500 Ridley Place.* I slipped it in between the pages of my little telephone book. It probably wasn't important, but

Miss Marple would've made sure to keep it safe. Then again, I wasn't any kind of Miss Marple.

A van pulled up at the side of the road.

Ricky leaned over and pushed the passenger door open. 'Need a lift?'

I climbed up and slid across the seat. 'My saviour.'

'Just been up to your Sheila's. She said ye were on your way home.'

'Thought I'd better get back in time to meet you.'

'And as if by magic — tad-dah!' He waved a hand in a mock bow. Shoving the gear lever into first, he pulled into traffic.

'Actually, I had to drop Joe off — he plays drums on Sunday dinnertimes with some old feller on piano. Up at The Engine.'

'The what?'

'Engine. It's a pub on Hexham Road. So I thought I'd pick you up.'

'I'm glad you did, me dogs are barkin.'

He laughed. 'What's that, London talk?'

'Nah, mate, dat's fackin merican, ain't it? Won't 'ear no Cockney boys talkin' like dat. Not wiv a rich an fackin colourful language like what we 'ave, ay?'

'Learn that from your London pals, did ye?'

I sighed. 'Got to do something to while away the time.'

He glanced at me. 'Not goin' so well down there?'

'Let's just say it's not all bright lights and parties.' I swivelled round to look out the window, hoping he'd get the hint.

Five minutes later, we pulled up outside Mam's and parked in front of the house nose to nose with a black Rover. I had no trouble recognising the driver—it was Inspector Walton, and he didn't look happy.

4

In the kitchen, I made coffee, and carried the tray through to the front room where I'd left Ricky and the inspector. They'd sat themselves opposite each other, like rival suitors, each staring at the floor.

'Here we are,' I said, cheerfully. 'No biscuits left, I'm afraid.' This wasn't quite true, but I didn't want the policeman getting too comfortable.

I sat next to Ricky and made a big show of looking all relaxed and nonchalant.

Walton pulled out his notebook and flicked through. He sniffed and smoothed a hand over the pages. 'We'll still need you to come down to the station and make a formal statement of course, but Ah wanted to get a few things clear in me mind in the meantime.' He looked up, mouth stretched into the semblance of a smile.

'Fine.' I glanced at Ricky, but his eyes were still on the carpet.

'Can you be more specific about the time you left the main hall and went to the toilets?'

Glancing at Ricky, I said, 'The band started their second set at nine, so it would only have been a couple of minutes after that.'

'And when you reached the outside toilets...?' went on the inspector.

'Well, maybe a little longer.'

'And what about the couple you saw come in before you went outside?'

Casting my mind back, I struggled to recall what they looked like. All I could see was the man's hand pulling at the girl's knickers. I shrugged.

The inspector made a face. 'Ye don't remember their faces?'

'Didn't you interview them?' I said, with a little too much condescension.

'We spoke to everyone present,' he said, somehow making it sound like an accusation. 'But we could only speak to those individuals who were still at the club when we arrived.'

'I see.' I coughed. 'Sorry.'

He gave a curt nod and looked at his notebook. 'What about the people who went down the stairs *before* the young couple came in and *before* you went out?'

I blinked. 'Don't remember.'

Walton edged forwards in his chair. 'But you did mention them last night, so...men, women...which?'

Closing my eyes, I tried to picture the scene—me standing at the top of the steps, gripping the wooden banister, the door slamming shut behind me, banging open again, then... 'They wore trousers.'

'That's all ye saw?'

'That's all I remember.'

'So they were men. Two men...'

'Well...'

He looked up from his notes. 'Well what?'

'I didn't see their faces and it's not like we're looking at a photo is it? I can't say for sure. I think they were wearing trousers.'

'Right.' He resumed making notes.

Ricky leaned forwards and tapped the inspector's knee with a finger. The other man locked up. Frowned.

'Seems to me,' said Ricky, 'ye're treatin Rosie like she's a suspect.'

'As far as Ah'm concerned, sir, everyone's a suspect.'

'But whoever did that poor lassie in must've been that last person to see her.'

'And your point is...?'

'Well...you must know when she died.'

'Must we?'

Ricky looked at me, then back at the inspector. 'Ye's had the doctor out, didn't ye? He'd be able to say when she died.'

The policeman inclined his head. 'And?'

Ricky shrugged. 'Well, unless she got murdered a couple of minutes before Rosie went in there, she could've been killed hours earlier and whoever did it would be long gone. So, Rosie canna tell ye anything ye don't already know.'

Walton laughed, though with a distinct lack of humour. 'We could do with a few more like you in the force. Aye, right on the ball, you are, eh?'

'Really?' said Ricky, looking pleased with himself.

'No, not really, ye dickhead.' Slamming his notebook on the coffee table, he glared at Rick. 'For your information, sonny-Jim, that poor lassie could've been lying there with her throat cut anytime between ten minutes and ten hours. That's how accurate the medical officer can be. Oh aye, right on the ball.'

Ricky cleared his throat noisily. 'Sorry. Ah didn't realise.'

Walton paused, shook his head. 'No, Ah'm sorry. It's just been a bit…'

A silence fell over the three of us. After a minute, I said, 'Don't suppose there's many murders round here, is there?'

He shuffled back in his chair and turned to face the window. For a long moment, he stared out, his face blank. Then, in a voice barely more than a whisper, he said, 'Tracy.'

Ricky and I looked at each other.

'Her name was Tracy Short.' His shoulders sagged. He pushed the notebook into his pocket. 'Twenty-three years of age. Reported missing six weeks ago. Parents are devastated.'

'D'you think she was killed where we found her?'

He peered at me. 'That's the sort of question Ah'm usually askin.'

'Was she?'

He made a vague gesture with his hand. 'Probably. Too much blood for her to have been killed elsewhere.'

'She didn't work at the Majestic, did she?'

'No, but Ah believe she sang there a few times.'

Ricky edged forwards in his chair. 'She was a singer?'

'An enthusiastic amateur, so her mother says, though Ah got the impression she'd rather her daughter did something a bit more traditional, like marrying a bank manager. From what I can gather, Tracy and a couple of guitar players had something going. Not clear on the details.'

He stood up. Brushed a hand down his overcoat. 'Can ye come down to the station tomorrow mornin? Make a statement, look at a few mugshots?'

I got to my feet. 'Yes, of course.'

'The Station's on West Road, near the bike shop.'

After he'd gone, we sat for a few minutes in silence, until Ricky said, 'I'll take ye down there, if ye like?'

'Aren't you working tomorrow?'

'Aye, but…'

'I'll be fine.'

I went upstairs, had a wash and sorted through the clothes I'd brought with me. Given that I'd only expected to be in Newcastle a few days, there wasn't much to choose from, so I pulled on a pair of dark green pedal pushers, a striped top and a light green cardigan. I heard Ricky making washing-up sounds downstairs and wondered if the domesticated-man thing was for my benefit, though I knew he'd looked after his bed-ridden dad for years before the old man died.

Digging out Mam's old shopping bag, we walked up to Ahmed's at the top of the road and found he had a reasonable selection of tinned goods, but very little that I actually wanted to buy. Ricky knew the place well and gathered together a tin of potatoes, a Fray Bentos pie, a loaf of bread and a box of Kellog's Cornflakes. Apart from the cornflakes, it wasn't what I'd been used to, but it'd do for now. If I decided to stay around for a while, I'd have to start going into town for my shopping.

On the way back down the road, Inspector Walton's words about the dead girl kept going around in my head. I wished I'd asked him about Julie. Maybe he knew of her missing-persons report, or more importantly, had some clue about where she might've gone, or what had happened to her.

Back at the house, with the pie in the oven, I

emptied the potatoes into a saucepan, and made a pot of tea while we waited for the pie to heat through. There were questions to ask and Ricky was the one to answer them.

Sitting opposite me at the Formica-topped kitchen table we'd had for decades, I began with the obvious one.

'I've been thinking about you and Julie...were you an item?'

'An item?'

'Don't be thick, you know what I mean.'

'Ah stayed at hers a few times. Nothing serious.'

'She wasn't still at her mam's?'

He shook his head. 'No, they'd had a bit of a fallin-out. About Julie singing, an' that.'

'And her place...where was that?'

He chewed his lip and grumbled a bit before answering. 'She shared a flat with another lass on Penn Street, corner of Scotswood Road.' He cradled his cup, staring at the tea. 'If ye stuck yer head out of her bedroom window, ye could see Dunston Power Station across the river.' He smiled as if this were a fond memory.

'And the other girl...?'

'Alma.'

'Alma. She doesn't have any idea where Julie might've gone?'

He let out along breath. 'She says not.'

'And you don't believe her?'

'No, it's not that.'

He didn't continue, so I gave him a poke with my finger.

'Well,' he said, 'Alma, she...she's a bit of a...ye know?'

'Slapper?'

He laughed. 'No. Well, aye, I suppose she was.'

'Was? She's not dead as well, is she?' I said, only half-joking.

'Rosie, just stop, will yer?'

'Stop what?'

He waved a hand at me, as if swatting an annoying fly. 'All these questions. Ah'd've thought ye'd had enough with that copper.'

I put a hand on his arm, squeezed it encouragingly. Keeping my voice low, I said, 'I just want to know what happened to Julie.'

Ricky took a long slurp of tea, stood up and emptied the rest into the sink. 'Ah've told yer. She made a phone call. She left. End of story.'

'You weren't in love?'

Resting his hands on the edge of the sink, he stared out into the back yard. 'Julie didn't love anyone but herself. She wasn't even interested in the band. Not really. Julie was interested in Julie.' There was a sadness in his voice I hadn't heard before. 'Ah don't know what she really wanted. Don't think she knew herself.'

The Julie I remembered had been excitable and

keen. She'd wanted to be like Judy Garland or Billie Holliday, up there in the spotlight, soaking up the applause. When I'd gone to London, she'd been the one who persuaded me, urging me to take that chance, to go for it, to try anything for an opportunity to make it big. And I'd known she'd jump into my shoes as singer with the band as soon as my back was turned and that'd been fine. I'd been happy for her. But maybe she'd changed. Maybe something else had caught her eye. I wondered if she'd known Frankie Fenwick. Maybe he'd given her one of his business cards, tried to drag her into whatever sordid world he inhabited.

But that was speculation, and I knew I'd shoved both him and Julie into their respective boxes, labelled and judged like so many people had done to me. Still, something about Frankie Fenwick gave me the jitters.

Ricky had got into a bit of a mood, so I told him to go home and that I'd see him the next day. He moaned for a bit then gave me a kiss on the cheek and left. Watching him clamber into the van and set off down the road, reminded me of the good times we'd had together, when it seemed that life was full of possibilities and we really could do anything we wanted to do. But London had pulled me up short, made me see that my dreams were just that— dreams. Maybe I'd been a fool to think I could ever escape the North East, and maybe I'd be a bigger fool to go back to the big city in the hopes of turning things around.

I spent the rest of the day moping around the house, going through drawers and cupboards, laughing at some of the books I'd read as a kid, crying at old photographs. Later, I watched television on a tiny second-hand set Mam had blagged from some mate of Aunt Vera's. Telly still held a sort of fascination for me in those days, as I'd never even seen one until I went down south, but what passed for entertainment on a Sunday evening wasn't anything to write home about. I fell asleep in the armchair and woke up a few hours later to a buzzing noise from the set. Switching it off, I went to bed.

The front door banged open and running feet clattered up the stairs, a girl's voice shouting, 'Rosie, Rosie, where are ye, man?'

I sat up with a start and fell out of bed onto the floor, banging my hand on the bedside cabinet. 'Fuck.' The same dream as two nights ago, only this time I could still hear the clattering on the stairs.

'Sheila?' No, course not. But the banging continued.

Pulling on my old dressing gown, I hurried to the front door, rubbing my eyes.

'Ah, you are in, after all.'

Blinking in the harsh light, I waved him inside,

glancing across the road at Ivy Paterson, nosy neighbour number one, and another woman, leaning over their respective garden gates, watching. I could hardly blame them—it wasn't every day a police inspector parked his big black Rover on this street.

'Sorry to surprise you, but there's been a development.'

I couldn't be bothered with the front-room-for-guests routine, so I led him through to the kitchen and put the kettle on. *Tek iz as ye find iz*, as Mam would say. I retied the dressing gown and pushed a hand through my hair.

Inspector Walton looked as if he'd been up all night—his face had a shapeless quality to it, like a badly-fitting suit. Fiddling with his inside jacket pocket, he brought out a bundle of black and white photographs, shuffled them as if about to deal a hand of poker. He laid out half a dozen across the kitchen table, facing me.

'Thought we were going to do this at the police station?' I said.

'Like Ah told ye, there's been a development.' He waved a hand at the photos. 'Take your time.'

I dragged my chair closer to the table, peering at the images. There were six of them, all head and shoulders, facing the camera, expressions displaying a variety of emotions from alarm and caution to surprise and contempt, as if they'd been caught with their trousers down while checking their bollocks for spots.

The men had a similarity to them—maybe all six frequented the same barber or had bought their clothes as a job lot of second-hand tat and shared them out according to height and width.

I tapped a finger on the picture at far left, a sullen-looking youth with a badly shaved face. 'He was at the Majestic the other night. Tried to chat me up.'

'Seen him before?'

I shook my head.

'What about the others?'

I studied the images again and noticed one of the youths bore a passing resemblance to Frankie Fenwick, though I couldn't see how that'd be important. 'No, not really.'

His fingers tapped on the table and I noticed the tension in his face. I guessed it must be hard for him not to point out whichever image he wanted me to recognise.

'No. Just him.'

'Shite.' He made a clicking noise with his tongue, then slid a finger under the photos, gathering them together.

'The one I pointed out…is he a suspect, then?'

'Been done for petty theft once or twice, but no, not really.'

'But you do *have* a suspect?'

He smiled. 'A good copper suspects everyone and no-one.'

'And are you a good copper?'

'Not for me to judge, is it?'

The kettle whistled so I made coffee, two sugars for the inspector. No biscuits—I didn't want him to think I enjoyed his company. We sat in silence for a moment and I got the impression he had a burning issue but wasn't keen to bring it up. I decided to get in with my own question while he deliberated.

'Have you heard of Julie Henderson?'

He blinked and his eyes drifted off around the room. Then, seeming to remember something, he nodded slowly to himself. 'Reported missing. Couple of weeks back.'

'That's her.'

'A young woman walks off into the night with her handbag, her keys and doesn't tell anyone where she's headed.' He paused, drawing tiny patterns on the table with one finger. 'On the face of it, she's gone of her own accord.'

'People do that, do they? Just wander off?'

He eyed me curiously. '*You* went to London.'

'That's right.'

'Parents knew where ye were?'

'Mam did, yes.'

'And if your mother hadn't wanted ye to go...? What then?'

'I'd have gone anyway.'

'Well, then. Isn't it possible Julie might've done the same?'

'She wouldn't have.' I said this with conviction but didn't quite believe it.

'Why not?'

I sighed. 'Alright, I know she didn't get on that well with her folks, but she wouldn't go without telling somebody. If not her mother, then…'

'Ricky?'

I coughed. Thought about it. 'I suppose so.' I leaned forwards. 'But she didn't tell him anything. That's the point.'

He looked away, avoiding my gaze. 'Young women disappear all the time. Often, there's a legitimate reason. When there isn't, that's when we get involved.'

'And what about that poor lass the other night? You lot knew she was missing.'

Ignoring me, he tapped his fingers again. 'Do you know Frankie Fenwick?'

'Met him at the gig. Nice feller.'

'Aye. What did he want with you?'

'A fuck, probably.' I blushed unexpectedly. 'Sorry, slipped out.'

Walton looked down at the floor, half smiled. 'You're probably right, though. I shouldn't think Mr Fenwick's much interested in anything that doesn't come under the banner of sex, drugs and a good night out.'

'So, he's like a pimp, or something?' I bit my lip. There I go, I thought, labelling people again.

'Let's just say he's a person of interest.' He sniffed and dropped his voice. 'Ah'd keep out of his way if Ah were you, lass.'

'You think he knows Julie?'

'Claims he can't remember, but she'd performed there with your mate Ricky, so it's pretty likely.'

We fell silent again, sipping our drinks. Then, digging into his pockets, Walton took out several sheets of paper. Printed forms of some kind.

'How about we do that statement?'

We spent the next twenty minutes going over my story again, with the inspector asking clarifying questions and taking it all down in long, looped handwriting. When we'd finished, he read it back to me, asked me to check it and sign my name.

As he stuffed the papers back into his coat pocket, I said, 'So what was that development, then?'

He looked at me, took in a long breath and let it out.

There's no way I could've known what he was about to say, but somehow I sensed what it was before he opened his mouth.

'We found another body last night, in the back yard of a pub on Elswick Road.' He paused, and I saw his mouth tighten into a hard line. 'Her parents identified her this morning. It's Julie Henderson.'

5

After Walton had gone, I ran a bath and slid beneath the bubbles. Topping up the hot water more than a few times, I told myself it would do me good to relax. Sitting around the house all day wasn't going to help me deal with the stuff in my head, so I walked down to the phone box on the corner and called Ricky's parents' house. His mam told me he'd be at work until half-five then he and Joe were going up to The Engine in the van to collect Joe's drum kit from the day before. Leaving a message asking him to pop in when he had a minute, I kept quiet about Julie — if Ricky hadn't heard already, I didn't want his blabbermouth of a mother spilling the beans.

Julie didn't keep in touch after my move to London and though I sent a few letters and postcards, her replies were only noticeable by their absence. Maybe she felt bad for taking my place in Ricky's bed as well as in his band. It made me feel slightly less guilty to think so. But death has a way of hitting you in the guts even if the person who died is someone who hasn't been a part of your life for years.

Checking through my purse, and accounting for the few pounds I still had left in the bank, I reckoned there'd be enough cash for another couple of weeks. After that, unless I went back to London, I'd need to think about earning a wage. Maybe Ricky's idea of me re-joining the band on a more permanent basis was worth considering after all.

I caught the bus into town and bought a few clothes. Not because I was running out of things to wear — there were enough of my old outfits in the wardrobe to tide me over for a while, even if they weren't terribly fashionable any more — but because I needed something to make me feel better. An hour and three new dresses later, I walked down Clayton Street and into the Green Market, a place where you could buy pretty much anything, and filled Mam's old shopping bag with enough food to last me the week. I bought an A5 size notebook as well, and seriously considered splashing out on a nice-looking fountain pen, but reckoned I wasn't posh enough for something so middle class. *Divvent get above yersel, pet*, as Mam would say — a couple of pencils would do fine.

By the time I got back to the house, Sheila had arrived. She followed me through to the kitchen and I put the kettle on. Turning around, I leaned against the sink and told her about Julie.

'Oh, Christ.' She jumped up and wrapped her arms around me, her dark curls brushing against my cheek. 'Eeh, Ah'm that sorry, pet.'

'Ricky doesn't know yet.'

She gripped my shoulders, as if I might fall over. 'Poor bugger. He'll be in bits.'

We stood there holding onto each other like human scaffolding while the kettle boiled, then I made a pot of tea and we sat at the table, staring at each other. I didn't want to talk about dead people, so I tried to think of a subject that'd take my mind off it. Then I remembered something John had said at the funeral.

'Did you and Auntie Vera have a falling-out?'

Sheila pursed her lips and looked at her cup. 'It was about the house. Vera thinks her and Uncle Maurice should have a share.'

'What the hell for?'

'It's the house they grew up in, I suppose.'

'Yes, and Granddad left it to Mam.'

She shrugged. 'Ah know that, but ye know what those two vultures are like.'

I thought about it for a second. 'They can't do anything, can they?'

'No. The deeds are in Mam's name. Ah checked.' She looked at me for a moment. 'Are ye alright for money?'

'For now, but I'll have to make a decision about…about the future.'

She nodded slowly, as if she'd been thinking the same thing.

We chatted a bit more about house-related stuff then she left, making the excuse she'd have to get Bob's tea on. I wondered again why she didn't go out to work, but it wasn't a topic I wanted to quiz her on. Not yet, anyway.

Ricky turned up shortly after six o'clock. I took him into the front room so at least we'd be comfortable, but I could tell from his face he'd already heard the news.

'It's in the Chronicle. Joe had a copy.'

Kneeling in front of him, I clasped his hands. 'Ah'm sorry.'

He nodded, lips quivering, eyes glistening. 'Losing yer accent again.' He laughed, despite the tears.

'Only for you,' I said.

We stayed motionless for a few minutes then I sat down opposite him. 'What else did the paper say?'

He sniffed, wiping a sleeve across his face. 'Just that they found her near a pub on Elswick Road.'

'Do they think there's a connection?'

'How'd ye mean?'

'Well, between Julie and the woman they found the other night.'

'Don't see how.'

'They were both singers.'

Ricky wiped his face again. 'The copper said that Tracy lass was only an amateur.'

'Her name's Henderson — she wasn't just some

'lass'. An' she might've been an amateur, but so are you.'

'Aye, Ah suppose.'

'And anyway, he also said she'd performed at the Majestic a few times, so maybe she was about to become something more than an amateur.'

'Could be. Ah did hear talk that Frankie Fenwick was getting into record producing. Maybe this Tracy was hoping for a deal.'

'Maybe. Inspector Walton asked me about Fenwick. I think he's a suspect.'

Ricky raised an eyebrow. 'He's got a reputation for being an arsehole, for sure, but Ah doubt he's up to murdering anyone.'

'Julie knew him, and so did Tracy.'

'Lots of folk know him. *You* know him.'

Ignoring him, I ploughed on. 'How did you guys get the gig at the Majestic? Did you have to audition for him, or anything?'

He shook his head. 'Nah. One of his minions, a feller called Mason, does that. They always vet any of the local bands that want to play there.'

'If Tracy and her band were vetted, and were given some gigs, they must've been pretty good?'

'Depends. If the gigs were just for them, then aye, definitely. But they could've been supporting other bands.'

Ricky picked at his fingers, chewed his lip. After a while, he said, 'So ye going back to London, or what?'

London felt like a giant magnet, tempting me back to that pokey little flat in Soho. Though I had a job to go back to, with a relatively steady wage coming in, singing with a bunch of has-been musos in between acts that'd make strippers and drug addicts look virtuous, wasn't my idea of stardom. But if I stayed around here, would my future turn out any differently?

'I'll give if a few weeks. See what happens.'

'So maybe ye could do another gig with us?'

I laughed. 'I haven't done *one* gig with you, yet.' I made a *might-as-well* face. 'If you're paying actual money...sure. Why not?'

He clicked his fingers and smoothed his hair back. 'Champion! Cos we've got one tomorrow night in Byker.'

'Byker? Jesus.'

'It's at the Prince of Wales. Corner of Heaton Road. Ye can do what we planned on Saturday. Ease yerself in, like. Again.'

'And how much are you going to pay me?' I said, giving him a sly wink.

He gazed at the ceiling, pretending to calculate my percentage. 'Thirty bob alright?'

'That'll do for a start.'

It felt good that I'd managed to cheer him up a bit, so I took care not to say anything else about Julie. He left a little while later, promising to pick me up at half-six the next night.

I sat for a while thinking about things and got to wondering if my barman pal Eddie Reid knew more than he'd let on. If he'd been on the bar the night Julie went missing, he must have had some contact with her. I decided to go and see him.

The bus got me down to the Majestic just after eight o'clock. A few folk were lined up outside, waiting to go in. If it turned out to be a ticket-only event, I'd be out of luck, but then I spotted a familiar face.

'Well hello again, young lady.'

'Mr Fenwick.'

He'd been chastising one of the bouncers on the door, but when he saw me, his demeanour changed. He waved the offending man away with a rude gesture, as if the poor fool had committed some blatant social faux-pas. Fenwick turned his full attention to me, towering over me like a giant ape. I didn't relish playing the role of Fay Wray.

'Call me Frankie, pet. All me friends do.' He leaned against one of the pillars and lit a cigarette. 'Smoke?'

I shook my head. 'Do I need a ticket to get in?'

'Depends why ye want to get in, bonny lass.'

'Oh, just wanted to see my pal Eddie.'

'Eddie the barman?' His mouth took a downward turn. 'What ye want wi' him?'

I coughed and looked away, struggling to come up with a plausible excuse. 'He's got some records he said he'd lend me.'

Fenwick sniffed and gave me a hard stare. 'Go on then, but if ye decide to hang around, let me know and Ah'll sort out a freebie for ye.' The way he said this made it sound like he'd want something in return.

I nodded, offered what I hoped he'd take as a genuine smile and slipped past him into the darkness of the foyer.

Before talking to Eddie, I wanted to check something. Heading towards the exit at the side of the building, I found the spot where I'd been standing at the top of the stairs when the drunken couple came in. A quick look told me what I needed to know.

I found Eddie serving drinks to an older couple at the bar. His face brightened when he spotted me.

'Couldn't stay away, could ye?' He passed a glass of whisky and a G and T across the counter and took a handful of coins from the customer. 'Be with ye in a minute, Rosie.'

I leaned an elbow on the bar and gazed around the room. Barely two dozen punters were in so far, mostly middle-aged couples in posh frocks and dinner jackets. On stage, what looked like a dance band were settling into their chairs for what I assumed would be a thoroughly boring evening.

The musicians all wore white tuxedos and I wondered if this kind of event proved worthwhile for the lovely Mr Fenwick, or if it was one of those kickback agreements music venues sometimes had to go along with to secure a gig with a name band.

A young woman behind the bar finished with her customer and sidled along to join us. 'Who's this, then, Eddie? Your new fancy-piece?' She winked at me and slid her tongue between her lips.

'Bugger off, Cindy. She's an old mate, alright?'

Cindy laughed and held out a hand to me. 'Just havin a bit of fun, pet. How ye doin'?'

She had a surprisingly strong grip and I got the feeling she and Eddie were close.

'Rosie. Actually, I just wanted a word with Eddie.'

She held her hands up as if in surrender. 'Ah'll just go and fuck meself then, shall Ah?' She laughed and patted Eddie's hand. 'Don't hurt him, mind, or ye'll have me to deal with.'

When she'd returned to her post at the far end of the bar, I noticed Eddie had gone a nice shade of scarlet. 'Girlfriend?'

He blew a raspberry and tried to laugh it off, but I could see I'd hit the mark — at least from his point of view. Glancing along the bar, I noticed Cindy still had her eyes on us, giving me exaggerated winks and making lewd gestures.

'Just mates,' said Eddie, sticking two fingers up

at her. He turned to me. 'What can Ah get ye?'

'Information.'

'Ah.' He coughed and began straightening the bar towels. 'Sort of information?'

I moved closer. 'You said you were here the night Julie disappeared.'

'Did Ah?'

In fact, he'd implied he'd been on duty that night, but hadn't confirmed that this was in fact the case.

'You know she's dead?'

His mouth opened. He leaned on the bar and stared at my tits. 'Aye, Ah heard.'

I clicked my fingers. 'My face is up here, pet.'

He coughed, mumbled an apology.

'I thought maybe ye'd seen something that night,' I said. 'Maybe spoke to her…'

He gazed upwards, let out a long breath. 'No, don't think so.' He hesitated, then, 'Ah mean, Ah did see her, just not to talk to.'

'You saw her go to the phone, then?'

He thought about this, eyes flicking round the room, avoiding mine. 'Aye, Ah think so.'

I pointed towards the side exit across the room. 'She went to use that phone?'

'Must've done, aye.' I could see from his expression he knew where I was going with this.

'So, it wasn't broken?'

'Can't have been, if she used it.'

'Eddie…' I leaned right over the bar so our noses

almost touched. 'The cable is hanging off the box. It's rusty as hell. That phone hasn't been used for months.'

He frowned. 'Really?'

'Which phone did she use, Eddie?'

'Aw, for fuck's sake...' He rubbed a hand over his face. 'He'll fucking kill iz if he finds out...'

'Who'll kill you? Frankie Fenwick?'

Eddie glanced around the room, then dropping his voice, said, 'There's a phone round the back, in the kitchen. But it's for staff and only for emergencies. If Fenwick thinks Ah let a punter use it, he'll have me bollocks.'

'So Julie used it?'

He nodded. 'She was only gone a minute.'

'And then what?'

He shrugged. 'Didn't see her again.'

'But which way did she go? Out the back, through the main doors, where?'

'Ah don't bloody know, alright?' He shook his head. 'Ye'll get me in the shite, you will.'

'Only if Frankie finds out,' I said, grinning.

6

I didn't want to go out by the front entrance and risk running into Frankie again, so I headed for the side exit. At the top of the stairs, I stopped, remembering what took place last time I'd used this route. But having no intention of going anywhere near the toilets, I took a deep breath and hurried down the stairs, pushing through into the alley. Directly opposite, the toilet block had been cordoned off with rope and a *Police: Keep Out* notice. Though still early evening, dark clouds filled the sky, the Majestic throwing long shadows all around me, like a promise of evil intent.

With no idea why, I had a sudden urge to have another look, another glimpse at the murder scene. Knowing further hesitation would shatter my nerves, I crossed the lane, but had barely taken two steps towards that dreaded doorway, when someone grabbed my coat.

'I wouldn't go in there, pet.'

'Christ sake,' I muttered. 'Nearly pissed myself.'

Cindy stepped to one side, folded her arms across a generous chest, shoulders back as if expecting an argument. 'So come on, then, tell iz.'

I glanced around, confirming we were alone. 'Tell you what?'

'What ye were sayin ter Eddie.' She didn't look angry, but her face had hardened, and I guessed I'd be better to stay on the right side of her.

Giving a shrug, I smoothed a hand down my coat where she'd grabbed me. 'It's not what you think.'

'Oh, aye, an what do Ah think?'

'That I'm after him, obviously.'

She laughed, gaily, as if the most amusing incident had just occurred. 'Oh, ye silly cow. If only ye knew.' She laughed again.

'Knew what?'

'If Ah told ye that, we'd both know.'

This was getting silly. 'What d'you want, Cindy?'

Her smile faded and she tightened her lips. 'Was it about her? The lass that got killed?'

'Tracy? Might've been. Why?'

She turned away. 'Nothin, just…Ah knew her.'

Intrigued, I moved closer. 'Did you work the night I…the night they found her?'

She nodded. 'But Ah was on the upstairs bar, so…'

Recalling what Inspector Walton said, I knew Tracy's body could've lain there for several hours. 'She wasn't in the club that night, though?'

'Didn't see her. Doesn't mean she wasn't there.'

'When did you last speak to her?'

'Who says Ah did?'

'No-one. But you have spoken to her?'

She ran her tongue over her lower lip, dipped her chin and gazed at me, her eyes sparkling. 'Might have.'

London life had opened my eyes to a world I'd never seen before, things I'd never have dreamed of if I'd stayed in Newcastle. Relationships weren't always straightforward. In assuming Cindy's interest centred on Eddie, it seemed I might've misread what was really going on.

'Were you and Tracy…?'

She stared at me for a long moment, her mouth open, a tremor in her lower lip. 'Let's say we were close.'

'Really?'

She dropped her head, said nothing.

I looked at her, watched her long blonde hair wafting in the breeze. 'Did she…reciprocate?'

Eventually, she looked up. Shook her head. 'No.' She coughed, laughed. 'Not her type. Unfortunately.'

I wanted to say sorry, offer condolences, or something like it, but nothing came out, so I switched topic. 'Did you speak to Julie the night she disappeared?'

'Julie?' She inclined her head. 'Never said anything about her, did Ah?'

'But you knew her?'

She sighed. 'Ah'd seen her a couple of times, at

the Bridge, an' the King Billy. We got on well. She was yakking to Ricky after the gig that night, and we sort of agreed to meet up later. Just for a chat, like.' She paused, glanced at the half-open back door. 'Then Ah saw Eddie letting her through to the kitchen. He told iz she wanted to make a phone call.'

'D'you know who she phoned?'

'Ah wasn't listenin at the door, ye know?' She sighed. 'Ah don't know who she phoned, but Ah know who she *might* have phoned.'

I wanted to ask if she'd mentioned this to the police, but a shadow loomed over us and I held my tongue.

'Hello again.'

Cindy jumped at his voice. 'Oh, fuck!' Grabbing my hand, she squeezed it, giving me what I assumed she thought was a 'meaningful' stare, as if sending some secret message. 'Eeh, sorry Mr Fenwick. Ah was just getting some air, an' that.'

He snorted. 'Aye, skivin more like.' He jerked a thumb towards the back door. 'Go on.'

Cindy skirted around him and fled up the stairs.

Fenwick looked at me, his eyes going everywhere, searching, assessing. Finally, he said, 'Making new friends, eh?'

'Just chattin.'

'Have ye thought about my offer?' He'd somehow slithered closer to me and I could smell his breath, a mixture of smoke and whisky. His piggy eyes seemed too small for such a wide face, but that cold stare held me fast.

Sticking my hands in my pockets, I showed him my blasé face. 'Didn't really make me an actual offer, Mr Fenwick.'

He smirked, but I caught the anger in his eyes. 'Slippery little fucker, aren't ye?' Moving back to the door, he held it open. 'Comin' back in?'

I shook my head. 'Another time.'

'Not got your records?'

'Sorry?' Then it clicked. 'Oh, Eddie forgot to bring them.'

He smirked again and disappeared up the stairs.

It felt like a lucky escape, though I couldn't imagine what he might have done, given it was barely half-eight and passers-by at the end of the lane would've heard my cries. Assuming I'd get to chance to scream, that is.

I needed to find out from Cindy who Julie might've called, though I also had the feeling the young woman had her own agenda. The way her eyes lit up when she looked at me had given me an unexpected thrill. Like Fenwick, maybe she wanted something in return.

Forcing myself to concentrate on what had been said, I walked away towards the bright lights of the main road, thinking about Tracy and the people who knew her. Then there was Julie. The place where they'd found her body hadn't been revealed, other than it being the back yard of a pub on Elswick Road, but she'd made a phone call at the Majestic on the night she went missing. Could it be the same with Tracy? Had she also made a phone call the day she disappeared? And if so, could it be the same person? And if both girls had made phone calls, were those calls expected, part of some prearranged agreement?

To find out, I needed to ask a lot of questions. Trouble was, I'd no idea of Tracy's whereabouts when she vanished and I couldn't very well go knocking on her mother's door poking my nose in, at least not while her daughter's body lay on the slab in the mortuary.

Of course, I did know someone else who might give me the answers I needed, so long as I could persuade him to share that information.

By the time I reached the West End, it was gone nine so there wasn't much chance Walton would still be there. The Bluebottle-shop, as it was known locally, resembled my old primary school more than anything else, and I had an odd feeling of déjà vu as I pushed in through the double doors. Inside I found a small waiting area and a wooden hatch in the far wall.

I tinkled the bell at the side and one half of the hatch slid open, revealing the face of an aging police sergeant.

'Aye aye, pet. What can Ah do for ye?'

'I don't suppose Inspector Walton is still here?'

'Walton? Doubt it. Not if he's got any sense, like.' He grinned and told me to hang on.

Sitting on a wooden bench, I gazed at the black and white posters on the walls — missing teenagers, rewards for information, community action. None of them looked recent and I wondered if the display was simply for the sake of having something to cover up the drab green of the walls.

I sat there for a couple of minutes until a door opened next to the hatch. The sergeant leaned out and jerked his head.

'Howay in, pet.'

Following him along a dark corridor, we passed three or four offices and the distant clackety-clack of a lone typewriter. At the far end, dull yellow light emanated from under a door. The sergeant gave two quick knocks and pushed it open.

'There ye go.'

The office looked like it'd been converted from a broom cupboard, with cardboard files crammed into a wall of shelving, and a small desk behind which Inspector Walton appeared to have got himself trapped among stacks of box files, handwritten reports and various other papers.

'I didn't mean to bother you,' I said. 'Just wanted to leave a note.'

'Thought it might be you.' He waved me in, indicating a small chair heaped with documents. 'Shift those onto the floor. Ah was just goin' to get meself a cuppa.' He raised an eyebrow. 'Want one?'

I nodded, and he eased himself out from behind the desk and disappeared into the corridor. As soon as he'd gone, I stood up and peered at the pile of documents. The one on top had Tracy's name written across it in pencil. Flipping it open, I skimmed through. The third page seemed to be the doctor's report. Something about the way the victim's neck had been sliced across, the direction of the cut and the precise angle. It made gruesome reading, but one sentence would stick in my mind about the killer's technique.

Footsteps outside made me jump. I slid the report back to where it had been and sat down hurriedly.

'Thought you'd have gone home, by now,' I said, striving to sound natural.

'Aye, chance'd be a fine thing.' He handed me a cup of coffee and slid back into his seat. Pushing away the pile of folders in front of him, he looked around for somewhere to put them, then gave up and dropped them on the nearest pile of paperwork. Whatever filing system he used, it didn't seem to be working.

Leaning back, he nursed his coffee mug and looked at me, waiting.

'I might have some information for you,' I said.

'Oh, aye?'

'I've been down to the Majestic. Talking to folk.'

Leaning across the desk, he gave me a piercing stare. 'And what would've happened if one of the people ye talked to turned out to be the killer? What then?'

'Well, I don't think it's very likely, Inspector...'

'Oh, well, so long as you don't think it's very likely, that's all that bloody matters, isn't it?' His voice had a hard edge to it, making me feel like a kid being told off.

'I'm trying to help. That's all.'

He snorted and shook his head. 'Ah really don't need a Miss Marple-type buggerin things up, so if ye've—'

'The statements you took off Eddie and Cindy...' I said, butting in.

He hesitated. 'What about them?'

'I think they might not've been quite accurate.'

'You're sayin they lied?'

'They may have...altered...the facts.'

He dropped his head, staring at his fingers. 'Go on, then. What've ye got?'

I told him Eddie's revised version concerning the phone call and that Cindy had agreed that this is what happened.

'For God's sake. Why can't people just tell the fuckin' truth.' He considered me for a moment. 'Sorry, not a good example of a professional attitude.' He laughed grimly.

'I think they're scared of that Mr Fenwick.'

'Wouldn't blame them.' He gazed out of the window. 'Ah'll get the pair of them in tomorrow, see if they can get their stories straight this time.' He looked back at me, raised an eyebrow. 'That it?'

I forced myself to slow down, to say what I wanted to say without pissing him off. 'I've been thinking about Tracy.'

'Aye?'

'Yes, and I think there must be a connection between her death and Julie's.'

'Oh, ye do, do ye?'

'Yes, I do.' My face flushed and I almost blurted out an apology for wasting his time but giving up now wouldn't find the killer. 'Two young women, both singers — maybe not professional, as such, but they'd both performed.'

'In fact,' he said, tapping a finger on the desk, 'they'd both performed with your young man. Tricky Dickie.'

'He's not my young man.'

He smiled. 'Have ye told him that?'

I ploughed on. 'We know Julie made a phone call the night she disappeared. So...'

'So you were wondering if maybe Tracy also made a phone call on the night *she* disappeared?'

I felt myself sag into the chair. 'You'd thought of it already.'

He chewed his lip. 'It'd crossed me mind.'

I blinked, struggled to think of something else that would keep him interested. 'Is it normal? I mean, for someone to kill more than one person?'

'Killing people isn't normal, bonny lass. Most murders are accidents, blokes getting too handy wi' their fists, using too much force. Premeditated murders are another kettle of fish altogether. And for one bloke to kill several people, well, that's unusual. But not unknown.' He picked up a pencil and fiddled with it. 'There was that feller just before the First World War. George Smith. The press called it the Brides in the Bath Murders. Know about him, do ye?'

I nodded.

'So yes, it's possible, though your connection theory doesn't have much of an actual connection, does it? Apart from the singing and the fact they were both young attractive women.' He shrugged. 'Not much to go on.'

I edged forwards. 'But d'you know if she made a phone call?'

The inspector rubbed his hands over his face. 'And where might she have made this phone call from?'

'Well, from wherever she was before she disappeared, I suppose.'

He frowned and seemed to be considering this. Then, grabbing hold of the pile of documents on his desk, lifted them onto his lap and began sorting through the files. After a moment he pulled one out. 'Right, let's see…'

I watched him scanning the loose sheets, checking details. 'Maybe it's…'

He held up a finger to silence me.

'Here we are.' Holding up a sheet of foolscap paper, he ran a finger down the page. 'Reported missing by her parents on Monday, 30th May, having not returned from a night out on the previous Saturday.'

'And where was the night out?'

He gave a small shake of the head. 'It wasn't the Majestic, if that's what ye were thinking.' Studying the sheet again, he nodded. 'The Fountain. Rye Hill.'

I hadn't expected that. The Fountain wasn't a pub for young women, even if there were a group of them.

Walton gave me a questioning look. 'Ye know it?'

'Used to. My dad went in a lot. Years ago.' Mam would send me down there to fetch him home. I remembered the noise on Friday and Saturday nights, the fights and the arguments. Remembered pulling at Dad's shirt sleeve, trying to tempt him away from the bar. Remembered the slap that always came when his eyes eventually focussed on me, and the jeering comments of his pals, each one a certified arsehole.

I pushed my fingers through my hair, patted my cheeks, urging tears to stay put.

'How old were ye?' His voice had softened.

'Eleven.'

'Aye. Not a very nice place, back then. Been alright since Johnny Beaumont took it over.'

I stared at my shoes, noticed scuff marks. 'Yes, he's a good man, John.'

Walton placed the file in front of him. He looked at me. 'Alright then, what would your Miss Marple do now?'

Wiping the back of one hand across my eyes, I said, 'Interview the women Tracy went out with that night.'

'Yes.' He sighed. 'And that's where it all falls apart. See, according to the parents, Tracy was to meet up with friends and go to the pictures. We talked to all the friends her parents know about and none of them had arranged to meet Tracy that night.'

'So, how'd you know she went to the Fountain?'

He ran a finger down the file. 'She was seen by a friend of her mother, a Mrs Edith Wilson, going in there round about eight o'clock. Alone.'

I knew Edie Wilson—she lived a few doors up from Mam's house. She wasn't the sort to tell tales. 'Didn't she think that was strange?'

'Course she did—but not wanting to embarrass the girl's parents, she didn't come forward until after the body was found.'

'And what does John say? At the Fountain, I mean?'

'They had a darts match on that night, so the place was heavin. Beaumont says he never saw her. Didn't see her in the lounge bar, didn't see her in the taproom, didn't see her making a phone call. Nothing.'

We sat staring at each other for a few minutes.

'But where's she been all this time?'

'Answer that, an' we'll be halfway to catching our killer.'

'Maybe I can help?' I said.

'No, no, absolutely not. Ah can't have a young woman roamin around asking awkward questions. That's my job.'

'But—'

'But nothing.' He waved a hand. 'Ah appreciate your assistance with those two buggers down at the Majestic, but Ah want you to stay out of trouble, alright'?

'Right.' I sniffed and stood up. 'Tracy lived on Elswick Road, didn't she?'

'Aye, very clever, but no clues. Ah've told ye — stay out of it.'

He walked me back to the front of the station. Holding the door open, he said, 'Ah'm serious, mind. Ah don't want to be hunting for your killer as well.'

I nodded and walked off up Westgate Road.

It was proper dark now, but the road had decent street lighting and I took care to keep out of the shadows. Of course, I knew he'd given me good advice, but there were things I could help with. The Fountain, for instance. There couldn't be any harm popping in to talk to John. Could there?

7

I wasn't so daft as to follow up my theories straight away. The bar would be busy at that time of night and I'd be lucky to get a word in edgeways. Best to leave it until the next day. Plus, it would give me time to think about what I'd say to John. After all, I couldn't go accusing him of anything. On the other hand, there was always Mrs Wilson.

I got back to Campbell Street twenty minutes later. A couple of bairns were playing in the road, kicking a carboard box around. Crossing over, I went into number nine. The lights were on downstairs and I could hear the radio.

Edie Wilson opened the door carefully. People round here didn't go making social calls at this time of night.

'Oh, hello Rosie pet, howay in.'

I followed her past the front room into the kitchen.

'Barry's listening to a lecture about European politics on the wireless. Some liberal wishy-washy rubbish. Getting ideas above his station, that one. Wants to remember where he comes from. Anyway, nice to see ye, pet.' She pulled out a chair at the table. 'Got time for a cuppa?'

I told her no, I wasn't staying. She sat down opposite and picked up a tea towel.

'Awful shame about yer mam, pet. They shouldn't allow cars up here. Accident waitin' to happen, Ah'd say.'

'How's your Susan?'

'Oh, she's canny, pet. Leaves school next year. Wants to work in a shop but Ah canna see her passin her exams, so God knows what she'll end up with.' She folded the tea towel and patted it.

'You heard about the young woman who got killed?'

She shook her head slowly. 'Eeh, Ah know. Isn't it awful? Just a young lassie an'all.'

I leaned across the table and dropped my voice. 'Thing is, I knew her. Tracy.'

'Aw, pet. Ah'm that sorry.'

I nodded, shifting my expression into one I hoped would convey pain. 'I mean, I didn't know her well, but…' I pulled out my hankie and dabbed my eyes. 'See, the police asked me to talk to some of the folk who knew her, and I'd heard you saw her the night she went missing…' I bit my lip, blinking away imaginary tears.

Mrs Wilson reached out and stroked my hand. 'Of course, pet, anythin Ah can do to help.'

'Is it right that you saw her going into the Fountain?'

She turned away, studied her fingers for a minute. 'Ah'm not one to tell tales, ye know?'

'Of course not.' I rested my other hand on top of hers. 'We're just trying to find out who killed her.'

She nodded. 'Well, Ah did see her. Ah'd been on me way to see my friend, Annie Davis. She lives just around the corner from the Fountain, ye know?' She frowned. 'An' Ah saw Tracy on the other side of the road and Ah said to meself, Ah wonder where she's off to all on her own.'

'And did you see her going inside?'

'Ah'd crossed the road to go up to Annie's and just before Ah went around the corner, Ah happened to look back and saw Tracy going in the front door. Ah remember thinking, she surely canna be meeting a man. Not in that place.'

'This would've been about eight o'clock?'

'Aye, pet. I got to Annie's just gone eight, an' that's only a hundred yards up from the pub, so…' She wiped her eyes. 'Poor lassie.'

We made small talk for a few minutes, then I thanked her and promised to pop in again when Susan was at home.

Back at Mam's, I made myself beans on toast and settled in front of the television, watching *Music for You* conducted by Eric Robinson. It wasn't really my sort of thing, but they had an American soprano on who had a nice voice. After half an hour, I got bored and turned it off. Sitting quietly for a while, I got to thinking about everything that had happened.

Taking out my new notepad, I scribbled down some ideas. Thinking about the questions I wanted answers to, I made a list.

Telephone
Crime scenes – where found? Where killed?
Fountain – why?
Mrs Wilson – re: Fountain/witness.
Tracy – address?
Julie – home address/flat?

It didn't make any sense for Tracy to go to the Fountain to make a phone call. We had a call box at the bottom of our street and there were at least a couple on Elswick Road. Walton hadn't confirmed that's where Tracy lived, but the Chronicle had mentioned the area. I might not know the actual house number, but it was enough to go on.

Could there be another reason why Tracy went to the Fountain? If John hadn't seen her, that didn't necessarily mean she hadn't been in. Anyway, I had no reason to doubt Edie Wilson's account. I couldn't recall the whereabouts of the telephone in the pub, so I'd have to come up with an excuse when I talked to John.

I went up to bed and made plans for the next day. We had the gig to do in the evening, but that still gave me time to do a bit of detective work beforehand. Gazing up at the ceiling, I remembered that I'd have to make a decision about my future. Stay or go, either choice would have consequences, and they weren't all good ones.

For a change, the dream didn't rouse me into consciousness, but a half-familiar noise lingered. It took me a minute to realise it had been the letterbox. So, that's what woke me, but I still had the feeling of having woken up earlier and gone back to sleep.

Daylight streamed into the room, blue sky peeping through the gap in the curtains. Dragging myself out of bed, I went downstairs and collected the mail. Bills. Something else to sort out.

I'd run out of milk, so walked up to Ahmed's and bought a few things.

'Moving back into yer mam's, are ye?' he said, totting up my bill.

In London, I'd grown used to having a degree of anonymity. Round here, there was no such thing — everybody knew everybody else. And their business. 'Temporarily, 'til the house is sold.'

'That's one and a tanner, pet,' he said, passing the items across the counter.

'You been here long? In the shop, I mean?'

He laughed. 'Ah know what ye mean, bonny lass. Why do Ah sound like a Geordie and look like a Pakistani?'

I felt myself blush. 'Something like that.'

'Sunderland, born an' raised.'

'Never mind.'

He laughed again. 'Aye, Ah know — not a proper Geordie.'

He passed my change and I picked up the bag. 'You didn't know a lass called Julie Henderson, did you?'

He shook his head. 'Read about her in the paper, like. But no.'

'What about Tracy Short?'

He sighed, wistfully. 'Didn't really know her, but she'd come in occasionally. Mostly to buy fags.'

'Don't suppose you remember the last time she came in?'

He scratched his head. 'Can't say Ah do, pet, though she did pop in one night a few weeks back. Seemed…Ah don't know…excitable. An' there was some bloke standin outside.'

'Waiting for her?'

'Seemed like it, aye.'

'You didn't know him?'

'Didn't see his face, but I noticed he had short hair, like a squaddie, ye know? An older bloke, Ah'dve said. Well, middle-aged, maybe.' He frowned. 'Ah knew it wasn't her fatha, so it looked a bit strange, know what Ah mean?'

'Yes, I know exactly what you mean.'

Back at the house, I had a leisurely breakfast, chose my outfit for the gig, then changed into a pale-yellow polka-dot skirt, a white blouse and plain blue cardigan. The day promised to be warm, though you never could tell in Newcastle, so I picked out an old grey/green tote bag of Sheila's and stuffed my raincoat in along with my purse, notebook and my new pencils.

The walk over to Elswick Road reminded me of outings to Elswick Park on Sundays with Mam and Sheila. We'd take a picnic and Mam would sit and knit while we played on the swings. Dad wouldn't be there of course — he'd be in the pub as soon as the doors opened, and if we were lucky, we'd be in bed before he got home. It wasn't until my tenth birthday came around that Mam started sending me down to the Fountain to fetch him. Sheila'd been lucky — by the time she was old enough to take a turn at it, Dad was dead.

There weren't that many pubs on Elswick Road, but I still had no idea where Julie's body had been found. Thinking about the story in the papers, I decided to check round the back of each one. Surely they couldn't all have back entrances where a body could be stashed?

The first one I came to — the Miner's Lamp — stood on a corner, with a large parking area directly behind it. The entrance to the cellar lay at the side, a square wooden trapdoor in the middle of the pavement, right by the main road. I continued up the street to the next one. Jammed between a betting shop and a newsagent, the Skiff offered no access to the rear. Circling around the block, I found the back yard halfway down the lane. High walls ran along the length of the back yards and included a set of double doors. Pasted across the padlocked entrance, was a sign: *Police. Keep Out.*

I moved further along to a smaller gate on the edge of the property—maybe the staff entrance. It looked open, so I tried the latch. As I reached out, the gate opened.

'And where d'ye think you're goin, Miss Robson?'

Adopting my best 'innocent' face, I looked up at Inspector Walton. 'Just popping in for a half a lager.'

'Aye, and the rest.' He pulled the door to behind him. 'What'd Ah tell ye about interferin?'

I coughed. 'You said not to.'

'An' yet here ye are. Again.' He laughed despite himself. 'Tell ye what, Ah wish my plods were half as keen as you are.' He pushed the gate open again. 'Howay in.'

I followed him through into the yard. Against one wall stood the expected outdoor toilets. Thick ropes had been wrapped between the doorknobs to hold them shut and stop anyone looking inside. Feeling my legs wobble, I grabbed the inspector's arm.

'You alright?'

'I will be. Just seeing the place where Julie…'

'Aye. Maybe you should go home.'

I straightened myself up, clasped my hands. 'No thanks, I'm fine. Did the killer…I mean, is it the same as with Tracy?'

'Ah'm afraid it was. But unlike Tracy, very little blood at the scene.' He made a tutting noise. 'Would've been dark, hard to see. He'd have been covered in it. But even if she'd already been dead, he would've had to be quick.'

'This where they found her? In the doorway?'

He pointed to the first door. 'Across the step, half in, half out.'

'She wasn't killed here?'

He inclined his head. 'An' how would we know that? Apart from the lack of blood.'

'Well…' I thought about Tracy and knew she couldn't have been there long, otherwise she'd have been found sooner. This had to be the same. Even if most men used the indoor toilets, anyone drinking in the lounge bar would've come out here, simply because it was closer. And it'd be hard to miss a woman's body lying across the step, especially with the lights from the pub.

'Whoever's doing this…well, he's got a system.'

Walton stuck his hands in his pockets and leaned against the wall. 'And that would involve…what?'

I pulled out my little book and found the notes I'd made the night before. 'This is what I think — he kidnaps them, keeps them somewhere, then kills them. Then he dumps them.'

'Why would he keep them somewhere?'

I gazed up at him. 'Don't think I need to explain that to you, do I?'

He smiled grimly. 'No, Ah suppose not. But it's not an easy matter to carry a body around.'

'He'd need a car, or a van.'

'Even so, the logistics make it difficult.' He started back to the gate. 'Come out here.'

We stood in the back lane looking up and down.

'Narrow lane, no room for two vehicles to pass.'

I nodded. 'If he'd parked here and someone else came along…'

'They found her on Sunday night at chucking-out time. There'd have been folk about, up and down the lane. And there's another pub at the end of this road. More punters. Hell of a risk.'

'Maybe he likes risk.'

'Maybe he does.'

I walked back into the pub yard. 'So why here? Why this particular pub?'

'Perhaps he lives locally.'

'Or just the opposite—suppose he lives miles away, wants to leave them somewhere totally unconnected with him and his daily life?'

'Excellent. That gives us the whole of Newcastle and the entire surrounding area to search for him.' He shook his head. 'Come on. Ah'll buy ye a drink.'

We went into the lounge bar. It was just after eleven and still quiet. The landlord glanced at me, then passed a sheet of paper across to the inspector.

'There's that list ye were wantin. But mind, divvent gan tellin anyone ye got it from me, right?'

'Cheers, George. Mum's the word.' He looked at me. 'Half a lager?'

'Please.'

'An' a pint for me, George.'

The landlord set about getting our drinks, a look of apprehension on his face. I guessed it wasn't great for business being the scene of a murder.

'What's this, then?' I said, peering at the piece of paper in Walton's hand.

He dropped his voice. 'A list of punters the landlord thinks are a bit dodgy.' He sighed. 'Got to start somewhere.'

We sat at a table in the corner in sight of the main door. I watched Walton studying the list of names. I still had lots of questions I wanted answers to but didn't want to come over as too keen.

'I've got a gig tonight.'

'A musical event. How lovely.'

'You making fun of me?'

He laughed. 'Wouldn't dream of it.' He tapped a finger on my hand. 'You be careful, mind.'

'I will. Anyway, it's only Byker.'

He rolled his eyes. 'Even more reason to be careful. Where is this gig?'

I gave him a cheeky grin. 'Why? You going to come and watch?'

'Might do.'

'Prince of Wales. Eight o'clock. Bring your wife.'

His smile dropped. 'My wife's dead.'

'Oh, shite, I'm sorry…'

He laughed. 'Nah, only kidding. Not married.'

I thumped his arm. 'You cheeky fucker.'

'Hey, that's, cheeky *Inspector* fucker.' He took a sip of his pint. 'No, never found the right one. Anyway, no point a bloke in my position havin a wife — Ah'm never at home.'

'Cos you work so hard catching all these villains.'

'That's it.'

We sat in comfortable silence for a while. Two old guys at the other end of the bar kept looking over and winking at me.

I gave Walton a nudge. 'Those two think we're together.'

'Oh, give over. Come on, drink up. Ah'll drop you at home.'

I almost told him to drop me at the Fountain but thought better of it.

Twenty minutes later, I waved a cheery goodbye to the inspector and watched him drive off as I pretended to walk up to Campbell Street. As soon as the car was out of sight, I turned around and headed for the Fountain.

Walking past the main windows, I peeked inside and saw a couple of men at the bar, but no-one else. Quiet enough for what I wanted. Pushing in through the doors, I veered left into the lounge bar and leaned on the hatch. Looking through, I saw John hunched over the bar, elbows propping himself up. He faced away from me, chatting to the sour-faced scowler from my last visit. The scowler clocked me and made some savage remark I didn't quite catch. I ignored him and called to John. Heaving himself into an upright position, the ageing landlord turned to look at me, a curious mixture of joy and annoyance etched over his face.

'Didn't expect to see ye in here again, bonny lass,' he said, making his way over. 'Thought ye were gannin back to London?'

'Haven't made my mind up yet.' I leaned closer. 'Have ye got a phone I can use?'

He frowned. I guessed he wondered why I'd come all the way down here to use the phone when there was a perfectly decent one at the end of my street.

'Aye, it's round the back, next to the bogs. Ye havin a drink?'

I didn't want to be rolling in the aisles before I got to the gig, so I asked for a lemonade. As soon as John's back turned, I skipped over to the door at the back of the lounge. The toilets were directly opposite, the payphone on the wall next to them.

Picking up the phone, I listened for the dial tone. It worked. I realised I'd been hoping it'd be broken, then at least I'd know Tracy couldn't have made a call from the Fountain.

Delving into my purse, I took out what I needed. Then, waiting for the dial tone, I pushed two pennies into the slot. Propping the matchbook up on top of the call box, I dialled the number — 22500. It rang. I'd no clue what I'd say if someone answered, but no-one did. I pressed button B and got my money back. It'd been a silly idea anyway, more than likely it'd turn out to be some Jack-the-Lad's phone number that he gave out to any girl who'd take it.

Back in the lounge, John hovered at the hatch with my drink.

'How are ye, then?'

I shrugged. 'So-so.'

'Ah see the house is up for sale.'

'Is it?'

'Passed a couple of blokes putting the sign up this morning. Your Sheila was in the front garden, dishing out orders by the look of it.'

I laughed. 'Yeah, she'll be kicking me out soon.' Having him tell me something I didn't know, made me feel a bit silly, as if I might've been left out of the conversation about what was happening in my own family.

'Make your phone call alright?'

'Oh, no. She wasn't in.' I grabbed the glass and took a long drink to cover the lie. 'By the way, I saw Edie Wilson the other night. Says she saw that murdered girl coming in here.'

His brow slid upwards. 'In here?'

'Yes.'

'Nah. Cops were in askin the same thing. I'd seen her photo in the Chronicle, but never in here.'

I studied his face for tell-tale signs, odd twitching, nervous ticks. But there was nothing. 'Weird, eh?'

'Aye.' He straightened up. 'That's not to say she definitely didn't come in, mind.'

'No?'

'No, it was stottin that night. Had a darts match on. But Ah dare say she could've gone through to the phone, just like you did. Ah'd never've seen her.'

Inspector Walton hadn't said anything about this additional possibility. Could it be he forgot to mention it, or was John spinning a yarn?

John went back to the bar to serve a customer. It was the Scowler. He caught me looking at him and rapped his knuckles on the bar.

'Eh, John. Got fuckin' women in here again, pal.'

John cast me an apologetic look. 'No law against it, Davy. What ye havin?'

The scowler glared. 'Just the usual—a pint o' fanny water.' He guffawed at this and a couple of the other blokes joined in.

His crowing laugh triggered something in my memory and a wave of nausea washed over me. Grabbing a chair to keep from falling, I took a few deep breaths, mumbled a hurried thanks to John and went out.

Standing on the steps, I leaned against the doorframe, my breath coming in short gasps. Now I knew where I'd seen that man before. It'd been twenty-three years earlier — the night my dad died.

8

The wooden post bearing the 'For Sale' sign had been shoved into what was left of the flowerbed in the front garden, and someone, presumably Sheila, had taped another one against the glass in an upstairs window. My bedroom. Thankfully, my sister had gone—I couldn't be done with her yapping on at me just now.

I made a cup of tea and sat down in the kitchen, writing up my thoughts on the visit to the Fountain. It felt like my head was too full—mixed in with all the information about Tracy and Julie, I now had this new revelation. Somehow, I had to keep them separate, do my old trick of hiding things away in boxes until I could focus on each one properly. If I ever could.

In a bid to help me relax, I ran a bath and allowed myself time to get my head where it needed to be for the gig. An hour later, hair done, face on and dressed, I sat in the front room going over my songs. Ricky arrived shortly after six and I got into the back of the van with Joe. Mick sat in the front with Ricky.

'Alright, pet?' said Joe, patting my shoulder.

'Back in the saddle, eh?'

'Something like that.'

The guys told jokes all the way to the pub and kept me laughing despite the crude nature of their humour. We parked up around the corner from the Prince of Wales and began unloading the gear. They'd put us in the back room where a triangular wooden stage took up one corner. It'd be a bit of a squash with all of us on there, but at least I'd be at the front.

With everything set up, we ran through my songs, by which time punters had begun to drift in. We had no dressing room, so hung around the bar and got a few drinks. I said I'd stick to Coke to keep a clear head, though the real reason had more to do with the memory of the last time we'd all been together.

By eight, the stools and chairs in the back room were all taken and a couple of dozen punters stood around the edges and at the door. Smokers were in the majority and all too soon, a light haze hung over the room like a cloud, making the air stuffy and catching the back of my throat. I asked Ricky to open a window near the stage and stood there for a few minutes, in an effort to calm my nerves.

The PA system was smaller than the one at the Majestic, and Ricky had concerns about the sound quality. He'd bought a new Shure Unidyne microphone which I really liked — it was chunky, almost big enough to hide behind. I thought if I held it close to my face, I'd be able to cover any embarrassment. Though, to be honest, so long as I didn't find another body in the toilets, I'd be more than happy.

I'd saved myself a seat near the stage to watch the lads go through their first set. They'd learned a couple of new songs I hadn't heard before, *Under the Bridges of Paris* by Dean Martin, and something called *Mambo Italiano*, which had a great bouncy rhythm. By the time they'd finished their set, the crowd were well into it and I felt more enthusiastic about doing my spot.

We had twenty minutes until the next set, so Ricky and I went outside for some air. I didn't tell him what I'd been up to during the day, knowing he'd be annoyed. Instead, we chatted about the house going up for sale and I told him I'd thought about renting a flat somewhere. This seemed to cheer him up. Joe and Mick came out to join us and we launched into a spontaneous four-part harmony of *Mr Sandman*, ending with us falling about giggling.

'Aye, aye,' said a familiar voice. 'Somebody's havin too much fun.

Ricky coughed. 'Inspector. Not doing anything illegal, are we?'

'Not yet.' He grinned and I was pleased to see him wearing something a little less sombre than his usual dark suit and overcoat.

'Didn't think you'd come,' I said, when the guys had excused themselves and gone back inside.

Walton watched them disappear into the back room. 'Didn't scare them away, did Ah?'

'Course not. We're on in a minute.'

'Better find meself a seat, then.'

He followed me inside and while he went to get a drink, I made my way to the stage. Gazing across the crowd, I caught sight of a familiar figure leaning against the doorpost that led into the bar. Frankie Fenwick. He grinned at me and raised his glass, mouthing, 'Cheers'. I wanted to push my way through the bodies and demand why he was there, but I knew it wouldn't put me in a good frame of mind. And anyway, I told myself, it's a free country — even Frankie Fenwick's entitled to go out of an evening and catch a live band. There'd be no point getting myself all worked up about it.

The band were ready to go, and Ricky gave me a 'thumbs-up' sign. He began strumming the chords of *All of Me*, and the audience who'd gone through to the bar, began to trickle back in. I caught sight of the inspector holding a pint glass. He did an exaggerated bad-dance move, making me laugh.

After *Bobby Sox Blues*, I took my place on stage and moved the microphone stand to a more manageable height. Glancing over towards the bar, it looked as if Frankie had gone. Or maybe he was doing the gentlemanly thing and staying out of my line of sight. Ricky held up his hands for silence, though no-one took any notice. Sidling up next to me, he grasped the mic.

'Ladies and gentlemen, boys and girls, we've got a special treat for yous tonight. All the way from the bright lights of London town, let's have a big hand for the fantastic Rosie Robson.'

A smattering of applause ran around the room, but it was Inspector Walton whose big hands made the most noise. I blushed as he winked at me and I pulled the mic back from Ricky, concentrating on the floor.

As Ricky's smooth guitar picked out the melody for the introduction, I felt myself transform into the person I became on stage—an exciting, more enthusiastic version of myself.

Though the crowd had been welcoming up to now, you could never tell what might happen when someone new appeared on stage. But I needn't have worried. As I meandered into the first lines of *Stormy Weather*, a roar of approval arose that almost drowned out the music. My whole body throbbed with delight.

After the gig, the bulk of the audience dissolved into the other bar, like a shoal of minnows searching for food. Walton still stood at the back, a big smile on his face. I'd avoided standing near him after my spot but couldn't stay away indefinitely. If he'd seen Frankie too, he didn't mention it.

'Ah'm impressed,' he said, when I finally went over to talk to him.

'So you should be.'

We chatted about the gig for a few minutes while Ricky and the lads packed up the gear. The crowd had thinned out and only a dozen or so members of the audience remained in their seats.

'Few familiar faces in,' said Walton.

'Really?' I said. 'Like who?'

Ignoring my question, he turned towards me, cradling his pint glass. 'Tell me something—is it usual for punters to follow a band around to different venues?'

'It's unusual for bands like ours, but if they're more well-known, then yeah, quite common.' I glanced around the room, looking for the *familiar faces* he'd mentioned.

Leaning closer, he said, 'It occurred to me our killer might be doin' the same. Following particular acts, particular singers.'

'Oh, shit. You don't think he's following us, do you?'

'No reason to think so, but it's worth giving it a bit of thought.' He looked over at the band. 'Ah'm sure ye're fine when you're with the lads, but ye do need to be careful.'

'Yeah, of course. I'm not five, you know?'

He dropped his eyes and seemed to be contemplating something. After a moment, he said, 'Another young woman's gone missin.'

I felt my stomach lurch and I grabbed for his arm to steady myself.

'Alright?'

I nodded. 'Just a bit lightheaded. Could do with a pee.'

'Ah don't want ye goin to the toilet on your own.'

I gave him a look. 'You goin to come with me, like?'

His face reddened and he wiped a hand across his mouth. 'Course not. Ah'm just worried about ye, that's all.'

'Who is she?'

His eyes searched the room, then came back to mine. 'Lizzy Johnstone.' He paused. 'She's a singer.'

'Christ.'

'Or at least she was.'

We'd been standing next to the outside door. It banged open, and a middle-aged ginger-haired copper looked in. Seeing the inspector, he muttered an apology and leaned over to whisper in his ear.

Walton nodded and told the officer he'd be with him shortly. To me, he said, 'Duty calls.'

'Bit old to be a constable, isn't he?'

'What, Thornton? Not really. Ex-army. Came to the force late in life. Good cop, though.' He squeezed my hand. 'Remember what Ah said, right?'

'Yes. And you be careful as well.'

He grinned and went out.

When we got back to the house, Ricky made cup-of-tea noises, so we said our goodnights to the guys and climbed out of the van.

Inside, I hung my coat up in the hall. When I turned around Ricky had closed the gap between us. His fingers found mine and he tugged me closer.

I unlinked my hand and stepped back. 'You're not staying the night, mind.'

He huffed and puffed out his chest. 'Wasn't expectin to. Not the only lass in Newcastle, ye know?'

I laughed before I could stop it. Ricky glared at me, then allowed himself a dopey grin.

In the kitchen, I found a tin of hot chocolate. I had plenty of milk, so I heated up a pan and filled a couple of mugs. We sat across from each other, stirring the lumps away, not saying much. I hadn't mentioned what the inspector told me, but I knew I couldn't keep quiet about it for long. So, after a bit of umming and ahing, I told Ricky, and as I knew he would, he exploded.

'Jezaz, Rosie! When were ye gannin to tell iz, like?'

'I just did.'

He let out a long noisy sigh. 'Jezaz.'

'There's no reason to think he's after me,' I said.

'Oh, aye? Maybe there was no reason for him to be after Julie and Tracy either. An' look what happened to them.' He shook his head, as if in disbelief. 'Jezaz.'

He calmed down a bit after that, and I asked him if he knew Lizzy Johnstone.

'Lizzy…?' He frowned. 'There's a singer called Little Lizzy. Sings with the Cool Cat Crooners. Could be her.'

'Might she have performed at the Majestic?'

He shrugged. 'No idea.' Then, taking my hand, he said, 'Ah'm stayin' the night. Ah'll sleep on the sofa. But Ah'm stayin', right?'

I nodded, happy to have my own private guardian.

The front door banged open and running feet clattered up the stairs, a girl's voice shouting, 'Rosie, Rosie, where are ye, man?'

Out of bed, I found myself careering down the stairs, chasing my sister's skinny legs, her favourite blue nightie flapping around her, fingers skittering down the banister. I half fell, half stumbled into the passage behind her, skidding to a halt and catching sight of my own eleven-year-old reflection in the hall mirror. My eyes swivelled forwards, dazzled by bright light pouring in through the wide-open front door, Sheila caught in a halo of white, her voice calling to me, 'Rosie, Rosie, come on! Come on!'

I sat up. The same dream as before, only now it had progressed. Looking down at myself, I saw my fingers trembling against my legs. What the hell was this? Some kind of weird ghostly message? A memory of some long-forgotten event? I lay back, focusing on the images in my head, but already they were disappearing, fading back to whatever dark place they'd come from.

Closing my eyes, I pictured that blue nightie. It had been one of Sheila's favourites, a Christmas present from Auntie Vera, along with a matching one for me in pale green (the only things she ever gave us that we actually liked).

Something niggled at the back of my mind, teasing and tormenting me, revealing itself in fleeting images and fragments dragged from a memory I'd tried so hard to keep hidden. Well, it could stay hidden, for now. That particular episode wasn't one I had any intention of facing up to. Not yet.

Ricky had been shopping. Bacon, eggs and beans sizzled away on the cooker and coffee and toast appeared as I pulled up a chair at the table.

'Aren't we domesticated?'

Ricky dished up the food and sat down. 'Comes of having a mam who went out to work at half-five every bleedin' day. Me and me dad had to fend for ourselves. Ah had to learn to cook, or we'd've starved'

'Hadn't you better be getting to work?'

He glanced at his watch. 'Ah can go in late.'

'I don't want you getting into bother because of me.'

He sighed. 'We talked about this last night.'

'Yes, and we decided I'd be fine during the day.'

'*You* decided.'

'Whichever. Besides, I've got things to do, people to see.'

'What? Like your new best mate Inspector Gorgeous?'

'You think he's gorgeous?'

'Tch. Ah was being sarcastic,' he muttered, waving a fork in my face. Stabbing a piece of bacon, he attacked it with his knife. 'Just think ye need to be careful.'

'That's what *he* said. Inspector Gorgeous, I mean.'

He chuntered on a bit longer about keeping doors and windows locked and to make sure I didn't go anywhere dodgy. I didn't tell him the dodgy places were exactly the ones I would be heading for.

After he'd gone, I got dressed and went through my notes, adding the information about Lizzy Johnstone. Only knowing what Walton had told me, I'd need to get a newspaper. I felt sure the Press wouldn't have been given all the details, but it'd be a start.

Getting my things together, I set off for the town centre, keeping to the main roads and avoiding the Fountain. I picked up an early-edition Journal at the newsagent across the road from Central Station and found a café where I could get coffee and scan the news.

The story was right there on the front page — *Newcastle Woman Found Dead*. There were two photos, one of *Elizabeth Johnstone (25) of Westgate Road*, and another of the Heaton Ballroom, where the young woman's body had been found. Reading through the story, I learned that a street cleaner had come across the body on Tuesday afternoon, dumped in an alley close to the Ballroom. It gave me a bit of a shock when I realised the place was only a few hundred yards from the Prince of Wales.

Looking at the photo of Lizzy, it wasn't hard to see similarities to the other girls. Like Julie and Tracy, she had long blonde hair, a nice face and was about the same age. My own hair veered more towards a pale ginger, but in a black and white photograph, I'd look almost identical to the dead girls.

'Hello stranger.'

I looked up. 'Eddie, you gave me a start.'

'Sorry.' His eyes scanned the headline. 'Another one, eh?'

I folded the paper in half, hiding the photos.

'Yes.'

He pulled out the chair opposite. 'D'ye mind?'

'No, feel free.'

Eddie clicked his fingers at the waitress and ordered a coffee and a bacon buttie. When she'd gone, he pulled the newspaper across and peered at it. 'Bit worrying, all this, eh?'

I nodded. 'You didn't get into any trouble with your boss, did you? From the other night?'

He grinned. 'Nah, it's fine. That copper came to see us, though. Gave me an' Cindy a right goin over.' He laughed. 'But no, it's all fine.'

'You don't know this girl, do you?'

He glanced at the paper. 'Heard the name. Think she sang with the Cool Cat Crooners. Never saw them play. Or her, for that matter.'

'Ever been in the Heaton Ballroom?'

'The Ballroom? Aye, couple of times. Saw Les Feeney and his band there. Wasn't really my sort of thing, though.'

'What about the Crooners? Would they have played there?'

'At the Ballroom? Aye, Ah think so.'

Eddie chatted away about this and that, but I'd stopped listening. I had places to go, people to see.

Mam used to bring us up to Heaton Park for a change once or twice a year and occasionally, as a special treat, we'd get to visit Clough's sweet shop on the corner of Heaton Road and Cheltenham Terrace. I'd always choose cinder toffee, even though it stuck to my teeth making it difficult to talk. Sheila invariably played the goody-goody and bought the cheapest boiled sweets.

I lingered on the memory of those happier days as I made my way down Heaton Road. Finding the entrance to the Ballroom, I climbed up the stairs to the landing at the top. Through the double doors I could hear the boom-ching-ching beat of a waltz. Peering through the gap in the doors, I spied a group of elderly couples gently circling the room in time to the music.

'Looking for someone, pet?'

A woman wearing a headscarf and carrying a mop appeared at my side.

'Oh, yes. I'm trying to find out about some musicians who might have performed here.'

'Ye'll be wantin Teddy. He'll be in 'is office.' She crooked a finger at me and led me along a corridor into a small room. A fat man in braces and a tight-fitting waistcoat busied himself doing two-finger typing on a battered old Remington.

'Young lassie to see ye, Teddy,' announced the headscarf-wearer. She gave me a smile and went back to her mop.

The man called Teddy looked up at me, sighed, and made a few humphing noises. 'Well as ye can see, pet, Ah'm right in the middle of summat, so make it quick.'

When I'd told him what I wanted, he leaned back in his chair. 'Give iz a minute, pet. It'll come to iz...' He closed his eyes, tapped the desk a few times then sat up straight. 'What's today?'

'Er...Wednesday. The twentieth.'

He held up a hand and counted on his fingers, tapping on each digit then folding it down carefully. 'Twenty, nineteen, eighteen. Aye, that's right. They were in on Monday night doing a complimentary show for the youth club. Didn't watch 'em meself, like. Pile of shite an' too fuckin' loud if ye ask me, but that's what the young'uns want, isn't it?'

I smiled. 'I suppose it is.'

He peered at me. 'Ah've seen you before, haven't Ah? Not here, mind, maybe down at the Bridge?'

'It's a few years since I was there, but yes.'

He waggled a finger at me. 'Used to do Stormy Weather, didn't ye?'

'Still do.'

He let out a satisfied sigh. 'Don't write 'em like they used to, eh?'

'No, they don't.'

He sat up suddenly. 'Right, is that it?'

'Er...yes, thanks very much, Mr...?'

'Go on, then, bugger off.' And with that he resumed his two-finger keyboard dance.

Back outside, I felt like I'd made progress. The band had appeared at the Ballroom on Monday night and by Tuesday afternoon, Lizzy Johnstone was dead. The next thing would be to find the place where her body had been found. Crossing the road, I stood at the other side facing the ballroom and the line of shops and businesses below. On the left, I noticed a narrow alley, about thirty yards past the Ballroom entrance. A piece of wood had been wedged in the gap to prevent rubber-necking nosy-parkers. But that didn't apply to me.

Crossing back over, I walked past the alley, checking for any police presence. Unlike the other murder scenes, no official signs had been put up, but a figure in a domed helmet marched up and down the alley like a guardsman. Moving closer, I recognised him as the plod who'd come into the Prince of Wales to see Walton.

'Hello,' I called, in my friendliest voice.

'Not allowed in here, madam,' he said, striding towards me. Then, apparently making the connection, he offered a friendly, though formal, smile. 'Miss Robson, ain't it? The inspector was talkin' about you.'

I took that as a good sign. 'You can call me Rosie.'

He nodded. 'Still, you can't come in 'ere. I fact, I'd better take a note of your…interest…just in case.' Taking out his notebook, he jotted something down, eyeing me suspiciously.

'Is that where the body was found?'

He glanced back. 'Per'aps.'

'With her throat cut?'

He stepped closer to the wooden board, so our faces were only a few inches apart. 'How'd you know that?'

I gave him a sly wink. 'I'm one of Inspector Walton's trusted collaborators.' Pushing my luck seemed to be working well. I soldiered on. 'But she wasn't killed, here, right?'

'Not for me to say.'

'But she wasn't. Was she?'

He coughed, eyes flicking up and down the street. 'Maybe.'

Peering past him into the alley, I was about to ask another question when he came smartly to attention and stared over my shoulder, eyes wide.

Turning around, I saw a black Rover parked at the kerb. Inspector Walton leaned over and pushed the passenger door open.

Glancing back at the copper, I muttered, 'Think that's my cue,' and climbed into the car.

The detective looked as if he'd slept in his face. 'Thought ye were going to be careful?'

'I am being careful.'

'You're a difficult lass to find. Ah've been over to your mam's place, up at your Sheila's, everywhere.'

'So how'd you find me?'

'Went to see our friend Eddie at the Majestic. Couldn't keep his trap shut about all your questions this morning.'

'Ah.'

He sniffed and studied the steering wheel. For a long moment, he didn't say anything, then, 'We've had a communication.'

'A what?'

He looked at me, and I saw the concern in his eyes. 'A message.'

'From him?'

'Looks like it.' He hesitated. 'It's a message about you.'

9

We headed back up Heaton Road.

'Where're we going?'

'East End Police Station, Headlam Street. Also known as the Bluebottle-shop.' He winked at me. 'That's what ye call it, isn't it?'

'Who me, Inspector? No, I think you're confusing me with one of the common people.'

He laughed. 'The cop-shop, then? That better?'

'We're not going to the one up west?'

'Just a precaution.'

I didn't like the sound of that, but he wouldn't say anything more until we'd parked and were safely ensconced in an empty second-floor office overlooking Conyers Road.

Walton went off to find coffee and came back a few minutes later bearing steaming mugs and half a packet of custard creams.

Sitting across from me, he rested his big hands on the table. 'Right.' Reaching into his pocket, he pulled out a long brown envelope and laid it in front of me. 'Someone left this under a pile of letters at my front office this morning. And before ye ask, no-one saw anything. Could've been dropped in by almost anyone. Slipped it in there when the desk sergeant wasn't looking.'

The end flap of the envelope hung open. Picking it up by the long edges, I held it between thumb and middle finger, squeezing it gently so I could see inside. With my other hand, I reached in and withdrew a single piece of paper, letting it fall onto the desk. The sheet had been cut to fit into the envelope without needing to be folded. The words scrawled in a combination of small and capital letters, as if written by a child, but the message wasn't difficult to read.

> *thRee dollS doWn*
> *MorE would be NiCE*
> *lOOk ouT RosiE*
> *oR your throAt I'll Slice*

Walton coughed. 'Nothin wrong with his spelling.'

'Oh, well, that's good to know,' I said, not bothering to hide my sarcasm.

'I'll take ye home with me tonight.'

'Oh, will you, indeed?'

'Aye, Ah will. Ah've let your sister know where you'll be, but Ah've warned her not to come over in case she's followed.'

My mouth dropped open. 'You think he's after

her, too?'

'Doubt it—singers is what he's into, but Ah don't want this fucker second-guessing us. Ah want to be ahead of him.'

'I'd better call Ricky.'

'Ah've done that. He wasn't happy, but there ye go.'

'What are you going to do? Keep me hidden away until this psycho hands himself in?'

'Ideally, yes.'

'Great.'

Walton told me I was to stay put until dark, just in case. Then along with a woman police officer, we'd sneak out the back way into another car and drive to his house.

'Where d'you live? Better be somewhere nice.'

He laughed. 'Ah'm sure it'll be good enough for you.'

'I haven't got my toothbrush.'

'It's all being sorted.'

If it wasn't for the threat of being murdered, I'd have felt quite excited.

The Woman Police Officer arrived about nine o'clock and introduced herself as Patsy. I reckoned her to be a bit younger than me and she seemed nice enough, though I could tell she wasn't best pleased to be stuck with me and Walton for the foreseeable future. She'd brought a bag of toiletries and a change of clothes for me. Looking through them I wasn't impressed.

'Why can't I get my own stuff from home?'

Patsy made a face and looked at Walton. 'Sir?'

The inspector rolled his eyes. 'Obviously, because we don't want a certain person discovering ye're not actually goin to *be* at home, do we?'

'If he goes round there intent on cutting my throat, he'll soon realise I'm not there, won't he?'

'Ah've told ye, Rosie, we don't want him second-guessing us.' He paused. 'What're ye smiling at?'

'You called me Rosie.'

Out of the corner of my eye, I saw Patsy grinning.

'An' you can put your laughing gear straight, an'all, WPC Fisher,' said Walton, flushing scarlet.

I began to think that being stuck with Inspector Gorgeous and his sidekick might not be so bad after all.

It turned out the inspector lived in an upstairs flat on Claremont Road, overlooking the south side of the Town Moor. After parking in a lane at the rear of the house, Walton turned off the car headlights and we sat there in silence for a few minutes.

'Are we waiting for something,' I whispered.

'Just being cautious,' said Walton.

The lane didn't have the benefit of streetlighting, so the only illumination came from a few lone windows in the bathrooms and back-bedrooms of the flats above us. Eventually, we got out the car and walked up the lane to the next block, taking care to stay in the shadows. I guessed this wasn't the inspector's usual route to his house.

Halfway along the lane we climbed an iron staircase to get into what I realised must be the ground floor of the house. Stairs led downstairs to basement flats and Walton told us to stay put while he checked it out. I heard him quizzing one of the other tenants, asking about visitors. A minute later he was back, and Patsy and I followed him upstairs to the top of the house.

The flat wasn't what I'd expected. Though not expensively furnished, the Art Deco sofa and matching chairs in a pale orangey colour went well with the more modern bookcases which lined two of the walls. It seemed Inspector Walton was an avid reader.

Seeing me eyeing the books, he said, 'Plenty to keep ye busy, though there's none of that Agatha Christie shite.'

'I'm shocked,' I said, in a slightly mocking tone.

'Ah prefer a bit more realism in my crime thrillers. Dashiell Hammett, Raymond Chandler, that sort of thing.'

'And that's realistic, is it, for a modern-day British detective?'

'In that the plots don't rely on a little group of

aristocratic landowners who happen to get shoved together for some ridiculous social reason just so one of them can start knocking off the others, yes.'

Patsy watched this exchange with interest, and I could see from her smiling expression that, contrary to my earlier assumption, she had a bit of a soft spot for her boss.

Walton slipped out of his overcoat and threw it carelessly across the sofa. 'You'll be in the front bedroom,' he said to me. 'Fisher—ye're on the sofa. Ah'll take the box room.'

'Am I being sent to bed with no supper, then?' I said.

His mouth dropped open. 'Oh.' He laughed. 'Sorry, Ah'd forgotten about food.' He walked through to the kitchen and in a few minutes, we heard him clattering about with pans and plates.

Patsy made herself comfortable, but not before checking windows and doors at the back and front of the house and jamming the front door shut with a chair. She seemed efficient and confident, though only being a WPC, I wondered how much satisfaction she got out of her job.

We chatted about nothing in particular until Walton came through with plates of pasta and some sort of meat. I'd expected egg and chips or some such delicacy, and realised I'd have to review my opinion of him. Again.

After we'd eaten, Patsy helped me organise my

bedding and unpacked the few items she'd brought with her.

'Don't suppose you've got a bottle of gin in there?' I said, eyeing her bag.

'Ah did think about it,' she said. 'Best not, though, given the circumstances.'

I watched her plumping up cushions on the sofa. 'You going to be keeping a lookout, then?'

'We've a car doing a drive-by, so we should be fine to try and get a bit of sleep.'

Walton had cleared away our plates. Now he came back into the living room.

'Right, so let's try and get some rest. Unless this feller's a lot smarter than Ah'm givin' him credit for, he won't have a clue where ye are. An' even if he does know, Ah canna see him shimmying up the wall and comin' in through the window.'

We were sitting at the table and I felt the excitement of earlier ebbing away. Now it seemed like there was just me, sitting in a police officer's flat waiting for some madman to come and murder me.

'There's something you haven't mentioned,' I said to Walton. 'Why did he change his routine?'

The inspector glanced at Patsy. 'Aye, Ah thought ye might mention that.'

'Well, he has, hasn't he?' I said. 'Snatching Lizzy Johnstone and killing almost straight away. That's a big difference to what happened with the others.'

Walton sighed. 'Ah can't disagree. An' Ah've no

idea why he's done it. But there'll be a reason, ye can be sure of that.'

'Trouble is,' said Patsy, 'there's no real pattern for this type of murder. Ye know, a string of killings, one after the other.' She shrugged. 'It just doesn't happen. Not round here, anyway.'

'If we knew what's motiving him, it'd help,' said Walton, tapping his fingers on the table.

Something that hadn't been talked about came into my head. 'You've never really said what he…what he does with them.'

Walton coughed and shifted his weight. 'Ah'd rather not go into that, if ye don't mind. Let's just say it isn't pleasant.'

That didn't make me feel any better and I knew going to bed with that idea in my head wouldn't do me any favours, so I suggested we play a game.

Walton frowned. 'A game?'

'You know? Like Draughts or something.'

He rolled his eyes, but admitted it was probably a good idea to concentrate on something else. A few minutes later, he'd produced a pre-war edition of Monopoly, which we all laughed about. Though I wasn't able to completely forget about the threat hanging over me, it did help settle me down a little.

An hour later, I went into the bedroom and got undressed. Patsy had brought a horrible nylon nightie for me, which scratched my skin, but did keep me warm. Lying in the single bed, I watched as the pale light from the window carved spooky patterns across the ceiling.

I woke up with a start, mostly due to not having had that awful dream again. At least that was something to be grateful for. Swinging my legs round, I stood up and looked out of the window. Across the road, the Town Moor spread out like a blanket, lush and green, dotted with trees and distant figures walking dogs, chasing kids, kicking balls high into the air. That's what I wanted — a normal life, a life that didn't involve dead bodies and bad memories coming back to haunt me.

I pulled on an old dressing gown Walton had loaned me and went to the bathroom. My eyes appeared slightly less dull and lifeless than I'd have expected, and my skin had glow to it, as if I'd been slapped several times.

Hearing the telephone ring, I listened at the bathroom door, but couldn't make out anything other than Walton's mumbling tones. After a wash, I got dressed and went into the living room.

Patsy and Walton were huddled over the table, deep in conversation. Seeing me, they shut up.

'Don't let me interrupt anything,' I said.

The inspector smiled. 'Sleep alright?'

I nodded, glancing at Patsy. 'Well enough.'

Walton pursed his lips. 'Ah've got a few things to do, so Ah'll need to leave yous here for a little while.'

'Unprotected?'

'Ah'm sure ye'll be safe enough. Ah've got a couple of plods on their way over. They'll hang around 'til Ah get back.'

'Breakfast?' said Patsy, heading for the kitchen. 'We've got cornflakes, porridge or toast.'

'Toast'll be fine,' I said, sinking into a chair opposite Walton. 'So what's this important stuff you have to do?'

'Remember when I showed you those photos?'

'Mugshots,' I said.

'There was one there Ah'd expected ye to pick out.'

'But I didn't.'

'No, ye didn't. Well, he was found last night. Throat cut.' He raised an eyebrow. 'Still alive, mind, but only just.'

'Christ. And you think the killer did it?'

He shrugged. 'If not him, someone with an awfully similar technique. Certainly can't rule it out, anyway.' Reaching into his jacket, he pulled out the bundle of photos from the other day. Extracting one, he passed it across the table.

Peering at the image, I recalled studying it in Mam's kitchen, but as before, I had no memory of having seen the man at the Majestic. His face bore a faint scar that stretched from his chin to his left ear. I couldn't help wondering what his new scar would look like. If he lived long enough to have one. Even so, there was something awfully familiar about him, something I'd seen before. Whatever it was, it'd come to me eventually.

Walton got up. 'Block the door when Ah've gone.'

I watched him go, then jammed the chair under the handle again.

In the kitchen, I watched Patsy making my breakfast. She opened cupboards, popped bread into the toaster, sorted out plates, butter, marmalade. She seemed to know her way around the place and I got to thinking maybe her and Walton were more than just fellow officers.

After breakfast I cleared things away, then Patsy wrote up her report, noting the time and that so far, nothing untoward had occurred. I wandered around the flat, running my fingers along the bookshelves, nosing into drawers. Patsy went into her routine, checking windows, peering into the street, noting each new entry in her little book.

I'd sat down on the sofa with one of our host's Raymond Chandler novels when I heard Patsy mutter something.

'Alright?'

She stood by the main living room window, looking down into the street.

'Dunno.'

I moved over to stand behind her. Though we

could hear the distant hum of traffic from the city, the street was as quiet as a Sunday morning. One or two young mothers hurried their offspring along in one direction of the other and the occasional dog-walker could be seen across on the Moor. But it was the other side of the road that had grabbed Patsy's attention. Positioned almost directly opposite the house, stood a lone individual, encased in a duffle coat with the hood pulled up to conceal all but the lower part of his face. As I watched, his head tilted upwards. He looked straight at us.

'Is it my imagination,' I started.

But Patsy had leaped into action. Crossing to the phone, her finger stabbed at the dial. Cradling the handset between her cheek and shoulder, she stopped mid-dial and muttered something that sounded like, '*Shit*'.

Back at the window, she looked out. 'Still there.'

'What's wrong with the phone?' I said, not really wanting to know.

'Everything.'

As we watched the man, he raised a hand and drew a finger across his throat in a gesture that made his intentions clear. Then, with a sudden spurt, he ran across the road towards the main door of the house.

'We need to get out,' said Patsy, with a surprising degree of calm.

She gazed around the room, ran into the kitchen

and checked the back window. 'Oh, fuck.'

'What is it?' I said, joining her.

'There's another one out there.'

Sure enough, another man stood in the back lane, looking up at us. He too wore a duffle coat, hood pulled over his face. As we watched, he walked towards the iron staircase that led into the house.

'Don't suppose you've got a gun?' I said.

'This isn't America, pet. The only weapon ye get as a lass in the police force is a decent pair of stockings. We don't even get to carry a bloody truncheon.'

Somewhere outside a terrific banging started. It didn't take a genius to work out that one or both of the strangers were battering the doors down.

'Right,' said Patsy. 'Time to leave.'

'Really, d'you think?' I said, my voice rising to what would soon border on hysteria.

'This way,' she said, and grabbing my hand, led me through the living room, picking up our immediate belongings on the way. I followed her along a short passage and into what I'd guessed would be Walton's own bedroom. Directly across from the door stood a double wardrobe, various ties and scarves draped over the half-open door.

'Oh, great,' I said. 'Hide in the fucking cupboard. That'll fool them.'

Patsy glared at me. 'Never read *The Lion, the Witch and the Wardrobe* pet? We're not hiding in it—

we're going through it.'

'Excellent,' I muttered. 'On one side I've got two maniacs, and on the other a mad policewoman.'

'Shut yer face an' give us a hand.' Grabbing one side of the wardrobe, she began tugging at it, dragging it along the floor. 'Come on, then, we haven't got all fucking day!'

I reached the other end and set about pushing it towards her. As the wardrobe slid along the floor, a door appeared in the wall behind it.

'You're joking?'

Patsy looked at me and I could see her courage was on its last legs. 'Used to be one big house. Adjoining rooms.' She paused. 'Don't ask how Ah know.'

Grasping the handle, she gave it a twist. The door didn't move. The banging downstairs had stopped and running feet told us the strangers were almost at the door to the flat.

'Right.' Patsy's eyes took in the contents of the room. 'There. Give iz a hand.'

She pulled out the single drawer in Walton's bedside cabinet and tossed it onto the bed. 'Grab this.'

Picking up the boxy cabinet, we carried it to the newly revealed door.

'On three,' shouted Patsy, above the crash of splintering wood that could only be the front door surrendering to the intruders.

Swinging the cabinet back, we hurled it at the door. Amazingly, the hinges gave way and the whole thing collapsed into the room beyond. Clambering over the cabinet, we ran across the room and out into a mirror-image of Walton's own flat.

Within a few seconds we'd stumbled our way down the stairs to the back door and were out into the open.

Patsy grabbed my shoulders. 'You're the one they want — get out of sight, now.'

'What are you going to do?'

'Now!'

10

I ran across the lane to the nearest corner, then round into the next lane and onto a pathway I guessed would bring me out close to the RVI. At the end of the path, I stopped to get my breath. A look over my shoulder told me I wasn't being followed, but I didn't imagine my pursuers would easily be put off. Continuing down towards the hospital, I spotted the Armstrong Building, part of Newcastle University. Hurrying across the road, I went in through the main door and almost collapsed in the reception area.

'Aye, aye, pet, ye alright, there?'

A uniformed porter leaned over the counter to peer at me. 'Ye needing a hand, pet?'

I asked him where I could find the nearest phone and he directed me around a corner.

Stuffing coins into the slot, I dialled the number for the West End station. It took a minute before I could get my breath back enough to explain what had happened, then a voice I recognised as that of the big sergeant from my first visit there, told me to hold on.

'Where are ye?' It was Walton and he sounded

panicky.

I told him and he made me promise to stay exactly where I was until he could get there.

I sank onto the floor and clutched my knees up to my chin. I was still there when Inspector Walton arrived with two plods in tow.

The journey back to Headlam Street didn't take long and soon we were sitting in the second-floor office again.

'Where's Patsy,' I asked for the third time.

'Ah've told ye—she's safe.'

'She's not here, though.'

'No.' He sat on the edge of the table, facing away from me. 'Ah think Ah know how they found you.'

I tapped him on the back, and he turned to face me.

'And?'

'Ah think someone's tellin him.'

'Someone as in…'

'As in…one of ours.'

'What? A copper?'

He shrugged. 'There's no other explanation. He's ahead of us at every turn.'

'You don't think Patsy…?'

'No.' He looked at the floor.' But Ah've put her back to normal duties.'

We sat in silence for a minute, then I said, 'And what about that feller? The one that got his throat cut.'

'Didn't make it, but he does have a link to someone else we've been watching.'

'Really?'

'Aye. The dead man's name was Arnold. Arnold Fenwick.'

'Frankie Fenwick's son? God.' I remembered looking at his mugshot and wondering why the face seemed familiar. Now I knew. He had that same puckered maw that Frankie had, a sort of cat's-arse of a mouth.

'Ah saw Frankie at the hospital this morning, and...' Walton shook his head. 'Ah can't believe he's involved in this. The state of him — he's a mess.'

'Well if it wasn't Frankie, and it wasn't his son, then who the hell's doing this?'

Walton swivelled round and slid onto a chair. 'We know now there's more than one of them, so Ah'm thinking maybe it's some rival firm that wants Frankie out of business.' He inclined his head. 'Despite being a total arsehole, he's got a lot of clout in the nightclubs and he's been buying up property, more clubs, mainly. Soon he'll be the only bloke in this town putting on live acts.'

Something clicked in my memory. 'Ricky mentioned Frankie might be breaking into the record business. What if he were collecting bands and singers ready to sign them up? He'd want exclusive deals. Keep them to himself. So if all his best acts were murdered, that would pretty much fuck things up for him.' I thought about this for a minute. 'But then, why pick on me? I've only been here a few days.'

'That's true, but ye have been pokin yer nose into things. Maybe the killers think ye're onto something. Maybe ye know something, or they think ye know something.'

'Well, if I did, I wish I knew what it was.'

There was a knock at the door and the ginger-haired constable handed in a note. Walton studied it and let out a long sigh.

'Another woman's been snatched.'

'Oh, God. Anyone I know?'

'Barmaid at the Majestic. Cindy Gibson.'

It didn't make sense. According to Eddie, Cindy wasn't a singer, and had no interest in the Majestic other than earning a wage.

Walton had arranged for Eddie to be picked up. Now the barman sat opposite me, a look of shock still etched across his face.

'Ah'm tellin ye's, Ah don't know.'

'It's fine for ye not to know something, Eddie,' said Walton tapping his fingers on the table. 'But Rosie here reckons Cindy might know who Julie called the night she disappeared. And if so, that might be why she's been taken.'

Eddie's eyes went wide. 'But how would *Ah*

know that?'

Walton shrugged exaggeratedly. 'Maybe ye don't. But maybe ye might've been listening at the door when she made the call.'

From his face, it was clear this is exactly what he'd done. 'Ah canna tell ye. He'll kill iz.'

Eddie had said this once before and I'd assumed he meant Frankie Fenwick. But maybe he'd been talking about someone else. Someone way more dangerous. I leaned towards him. and took his hands in mine. 'Come on, Eddie. Whoever it is already knows you've been picked up by the cops, so he's probably going to kill you anyway.'

A glance at Walton told me this was far from ethical, but he said nothing and we both looked at Eddie.

Dropping his head, Eddie stared at the floor. 'There's this bloke, used to work for Billy Hill.'

'Who's Billy Hill?'

The inspector stiffened. 'London gangster.' To Eddie, he said, 'What's this man's name?'

'Really, Ah canna tell yer.'

Walton stood up. 'Fine. You're free to go.'

Eddie stared at him. 'Ye what?'

'Free to go. Thanks for your help.'

The colour slid from Eddie's face as if we'd turned on a tap. 'But he'll kill me.'

'If ye don't know anything, there's nothing to worry about, is there?'

'But…'

'But what, Eddie?' Walton leaned down, hands splayed either side of the trembling barman.

Eddie's head swivelled from side to side, but his mouth let him down. 'Bernard Box.'

Walton snorted. 'Cardboard Box? Ye're fuckin' jokin'? He couldn't organise anything like this.'

Eddie shook his head again. 'No, no, it's not him so much. It's his lad, Charlie.'

'Ah.' Walton sat back down. 'Charlie Box. Known as the Liquorice Kid, cos he does allsorts.'

I laughed at that, but Walton's face remained hard. 'What else?'

'That's all Ah know.'

Walton persuaded Eddie that a stay in the cells for a few nights would be the best way to avoid getting his head separated from his body. Eddie scarcely protested and the ginger-haired plod took him downstairs.

'Why would Julie call that feller Box?'

Walton's head moved from side to side. 'Not a clue.'

'I mean, if he's like, a gangster, how would she even know him?'

'Again…' He held out his hands in a gesture of bewilderment.

'So what now?' I said.

Elbows on the table, Walton dropped his head.

'Christ knows.' He chewed his lip. 'Even if we organise a raid on Bernie Box's place, who's to say some fucker won't tip him off?'

'You still think one of your lot is an insider, then?'

'Who knew where ye were going to be last night?'

'Me, you, Patsy…'

'It's not Patsy.'

I nodded. 'Alright then, so who else could've known?'

'Huh. The force is crammed with folk that'll take a backhander for a few quid. It's not as bad as London, but it happens. That ginger bugger, Thornton—he's always short of a few bob. An' Ah'll tell ye summat else…' His head began to nod. 'Aye, it was him that booked out the car.'

'But how would he know where we were going?'

'No idea, but let's be honest—where else could we have gone? Another station? No, in his position, I would've said the same if I'd had to guess.'

'What about…is it possible to get the people you need to carry out the raid but not tell them anything? Would that work?'

He laughed. 'Aye, we'll just get a gang of cops together, armed with nothing more than a few bits of wood and a couple of fuckin' police whistles and not tell them what the hell they're going into and hope no-one gets blown the fuck away. Aye, it'll be fine.'

'Got a better idea?'

He sighed noisily. 'It could work, Ah'll give ye that. Risky, though.' He tapped his fingers, staring out the window. 'Aye, it could work.'

'Where does this Box bloke hang out?'

'He's got a yard under the staiths at Dunston. Had three of four men working for him last Ah heard.' He gave me a funny look. 'Can ye drive a van?'

An hour later, we'd picked up two Morris vans from the police storage yard in Byker and parked them round the back of the station. Walton said he wanted to keep me safe, where he could see me, and that included not leaving me alone at the police station — which I had to admit, didn't fill me with confidence. He told me to lock the doors and stay where I was in the driving seat of the second van, while he organised the troops. He'd already called in three patrol cars, putting out a story of a tip-off about a bank raid.

I watched eight male officers emerge from the back of the station, their faces displaying bemused expressions. Apart from Thornton, our ginger-haired pal, who looked as if he'd just been given a rectal examination.

'What's with the Black Maria?' said one young plod, climbing into my van.

'That's for me to know and you to find out,' I said.

He stared at me. 'Hang on — who the hell are you?'

'Van driver,' I said. 'In the back, please.'

Another three officers climbed in after him, all giving me funny looks. Walton got his own van loaded up then walked over and leaned in at my offside door.

'Right lads, this is Miss Robson. She's one of our volunteer drivers, so if anythin' happens to her, Ah'll hold you lot responsible, right?'

They all nodded.

'Now, we're off to pick up Bernie Box and his crew, so as soon as we're in there, Ah want anyone on the premises rounded up and in the vans as quick as ye like. We're particularly interested in Charlie Box and Ah'm sure Ah don't need to tell ye, he's a dangerous sod, so no heroics. Right?'

Walton gave me a wide grin and slid the door shut.

Following the inspector's van down to the High-Level Bridge, I felt quite important, though a feeling of trepidation had crept into my guts. If the raid went wrong, we'd all be in trouble.

Once over the river, we headed for Dunston. Within ten minutes, I could see the staiths stretching out into the tidal basin. About six hundred yards long, it was a sort of wooden pier, used to load coal onto collier ships on the Tyne. Around the area beneath the pier were various businesses connected with the shipping and coal industries. Bernie Box, according to Walton, was a chancer who'd taken over a failing packaging company and now used it as a base for his criminal empire.

Walton's van trundled down a rough track towards the river, curving round into a fenced-off area. The van pulled up near an opening in the fence and out of sight of most of the buildings beyond it. Walton jumped out and ran over to my window.

'Right, lads and lasses, straight through here like a dose of salts. Box's depot is the one nearest the river.'

Back in his van, he set off at speed and I followed through onto a patch of rough ground where trucks and bits of machinery were dotted about here and there. Seconds later we all piled out and ran to the three sheds that bordered the riverbank. Above us, coal trucks shunted along the pier towards waiting ships, the clanking and grinding of their wheels, ringing in my ears.

The officers kicked down doors and piled into the buildings, shouting and waving truncheons. Within seconds it was chaos, with police and thuggish-looking men at each other's throats. But the gang were easily outnumbered and as I watched, three middle-aged men and an older bloke were manhandled into the vans.

Walton came over to where I stood.

'Charlie's missing.'

This wasn't what I wanted to hear. 'So what do we do now?'

He waved a hand at the larger of the sheds. 'That place is stuffed with stolen gear. If nothing else, we've got enough to hold them for a few days.' He beckoned to one of the plods. 'Cochran — take two of the lads and go through everything, starting with the one on the end. And don't go tramping about in your size nines like a bull in a teashop, there might be a young lassie stashed away somewhere.'

The man hurried off. Walton jerked his head at me, and I followed him into the nearest shed.

Inside, there was a desk at one end piled with boxes and odd bits of electrical equipment. Wooden crates and stacks of cardboard boxes stood in the corner. A couple of filing cabinets and cupboards filled the rest of the space. The place had an unappealing smell about it too, a sort of heady mix of rotten meat and dog shit. And weirdly, dead flies lay all over the stained flooring.

'Seem to recall this was Bernie's office at one time,' said Walton, sniffing suspiciously. He gazed around. 'More of a storage shed now, by the looks of it.' He began opening boxes, drawers and anything that might contain incriminating information or stolen goods. The first box he opened held a dozen bottles of Irish whiskey. Walton made a note of it and stacked them by the door. 'Why don't you check that out?' he said, pointing to a wooden cupboard behind the desk.

The cupboard would've served well as a wardrobe for a very small person. It had been wedged fast behind the desk and I had to drag the corner to one side to make space to squeeze in to get at the doors. A small lock held the doors shut, but realising it wouldn't take much to break it, I gave one of the doors a sharp tug. It flew open. A woman's body tumbled out onto the floor.

11

At least this time I didn't scream. But my stomach refused to hang onto its contents, and dashing through the door, I threw my guts up outside.

I heard the inspector let out a mournful groan. Then he was at my side, holding my shoulders, pulling me upright.

'It's not Cindy.'

Wiping my mouth, I looked up at him. 'I know. But she's so...'

He nodded slowly. 'Aye, she's been in there a while.'

The body had been wrapped in strips of rubber sheeting, and only her clothing revealed her to be a young woman.

'Cochran!'

The young copper came running. 'Sir?'

'We've got a body. See if ye can find a phone and do the necessaries.'

'Yes sir.' He hesitated. 'The necessaries?'

Walton rolled his eyes. 'Doctor, Ambulance, CID.'

The officer departed and Walton led me back to the van, made sure I was comfortable in the passenger seat and went off to supervise the murder scene and the collecting of evidence. I sat there watching as the police did their job. Even our alleged spy, Ginger-nut, seemed to be pulling his weight and I wondered if maybe we'd jumped the gun in suspecting him.

About half an hour later, two more police vans turned up, disgorging a horde of officers into the yard. As I watched them getting to work, Walton came over.

'Think Ah know who she is,' he said, nodding towards the shed. 'Jeanie Little. Went missing about a year ago. Parents thought she'd run off to London, but they never heard from her.' He shook his head. 'Now we know why.'

'Was she a singer as well?'

He looked away. Seemed to be considering his answer. Eventually, he said, 'Aye, Ah'm afraid she was.'

It was after six when we arrived at the police station on West Road. The desk sergeant recognised me and from his face, I saw he knew about the dead woman.

I followed Walton along to his office where he made me coffee and found some biscuits. Sinking into his chair, I could see how tired he must be.

'You should go home,' I said.

'So should you, lass.'

'Where am I going to go? Back to yours?' He laughed at this but I could tell he knew I was only half joking.

'No. I think it's safe to go to your Mam's place.'

'With that killer still on the loose?'

'Bernie Box assured me his son is in London, so Ah made a couple of calls to a pal in the Met. It seems young Charlie's been under observation in Kilburn. Christ knows why he's there, but if he *is* there, he can't be here.'

'Fine. Can I have a gun, then? Just in case?'

'Ah spoke to Ricky. Ah expect he'll want to see you. And Ah talked to your sister. Your brother-in-law's on his way down to pick you up. Ah suggested your Sheila might stay with you tonight.'

'I see.'

He patted my hand. 'Ah've also arranged for a car to do the rounds up there every half hour, so there's no reason for you to worry.'

'A car doing the rounds? Didn't help last time, did it?'

'It'll be fine.'

'Right.' I coughed. 'So if Ah wake up wi' me fuckin' throat cut, that's all fuckin' fine then?'

He smiled. 'What happened to your posh accent?'

'Ah tend to fuckin' lose it when me life's in danger. Pet.' But I couldn't stay angry with him and I knew he wouldn't send me home if he really thought it wasn't safe.

Bob and Sheila arrived shortly afterwards and made a big fuss of hugging me and stroking my face as if I were a pet poodle. Sheila held my hand as Walton escorted us back to the car.

'Ah'll pop in tomorrow,' he said, as Bob bundled me into the back seat of his Austin A30 — a car that said more about Bob than it did about anything else.

We pulled up outside Mam's and sat there for a minute until the neighbours all went back into their houses.

'Nosy buggers,' muttered Sheila, getting out of the car. Bob helped with the bags, which, it turned out were mostly full of food, then kissed us both goodnight and went home to his television and fish'n'chip supper. He'd farmed the kids out to a friend in the expectation of it being a late night. I almost envied him the luxury of his boring little life. But that was just me putting folk in boxes again. Sooner or later, I'd have to sort out my own little boxes, once and for all.

It had turned cold, and I spent a good few minutes making up the fire in the front room. When it got going, it warmed the place up nicely, and reminded me of all those long winter nights when it was just me, Sheila and Mam, sitting round the fire, listening to the radio, pretending it was a special occasion.

Sheila bustled around making tea, whipping up

plates of sausage and mash. We sat with trays on our knees as if we'd not a care in the world, watching some crap on television.

Sheila didn't say much, but I guessed she'd have lots of questions. When she'd cleared things away, she brought out a bottle of port she'd 'borrowed' from Bob's secret stash and poured out two large tumblers.

'Here's to you, pet,' she said, clinking my glass.

A knock at the door startled me, but it was only Ricky. Sheila let him in and he gave me a chaste kiss on the cheek.

'Ye're alright, then?' he said, looking me up and down.

'I'm fine. Just tired.' I realised this sounded a bit like an excuse, so added, 'but it's nice to see you.'

He grinned. 'Got another gig lined up at the Majestic. Next Saturday.'

'Right.'

He coughed. 'Ah mean, if you're feeling alright about the place, ye know?'

'We'll see, Ricky. I'm not sure what I'm going to do. About everything.'

He looked hurt, so I told Sheila what a brilliant guitar player he was and how her and Bob should come to one of the gigs.

We chatted for a while longer like two people who don't really know each other, then he left, promising to look in the next day.

Sheila and I stayed up until around ten o'clock by which time, in bits and pieces, I'd revealed the various excitements of the last few days.

'Christ, pet, ye've been through the mill, eh?'

We'd gone around the house checking windows, closing curtains and jamming kitchen chairs against the front and back doors. Peeking out the front windows, I'd seen a cop car trundle past a couple of times, so at least I knew they were out there, if not right outside my door.

'Ah'll stay in my old room,' said Sheila. 'Ah'll leave me bedroom door open an'all, in case ye have one of your dreams.'

I stared at her. 'What dreams?'

She scratched her neck. 'Well, ye know? Those dreams ye used to have.'

'Oh.' I sniffed and looked away. 'Didn't think you'd remember that.'

'Hardly forget, pet. Ye used to scream the place down some nights.' She gave me a pitying look. 'Remember? We used to tell Mam ye'd been reading too many of those ghost stories.'

I remembered the dreams well enough but hadn't grasped that anyone else might have, too. For the first time, it occurred to me that the dreams had stopped when I went to London. And now they were back. But only here, in this house. Where it all began.

In bed, I lay for hours, not wanting to close my

eyes, wishing Inspector Gorgeous had taken me back to his place. But that was silly. He had his own life to lead and there was obviously something going on with him and Patsy. I should just stay out of it. Anyway, it wasn't as if I'd definitely decided to stay around…

The front door bangs open and running feet clatter up the stairs. A girl's voice shouts, 'Rosie, Rosie, where are ye, man?'

Downstairs already, I'm in the hallway and catch sight of my eleven-year-old reflection in the mirror. Then I'm dazzled by the bright light pouring in through the wide-open front door, Sheila in an angelic halo of white, her voice calling to me, 'Rosie, Rosie, come on! Come on!'

Then I'm in the street, running after my sister, bare feet stinging and sore from the freezing cobbles. And I'm crashing into Sheila, bent over something at the corner of the lane, something human, something man-shaped, something Dad-shaped.

I sat up, gulping in air, panting, sweat pouring out of me like a tidal wave.

Jesus wept.

Light flickered in through the half-open curtains. The bedroom door stood open, Sheila leaning in, partly-dressed, staring at me like I'd grown three heads.

'Ye alright, pet?' She sat on the bed, took my hand. 'Heard ye making a noise. Sort of moaning, an' that.'

'I'm fine. Just a…just a dream.'

She made a face. 'What'd Ah tell ye?'

'I'm fine, pet. It wasn't like a nightmare.'

True enough, I thought. This is more than any normal nightmare. This is the past come back to plague me, big time.

'Sure?'

I nodded, unwilling to get into any discussion about it, and definitely not with my sister.

'Yes, I just need a minute.' I gave her what I hoped was a relaxed smile and she went out.

So, there it was—the nightmare festering away in the depths of my memory for years, had finally made it back into a form that had some logic to it. But it wasn't only the memory of my dead Dad that I'd pushed away as if it had never happened, but the events leading up to that moment. The face of the scowling man was there too, and I knew it was time to consciously think about it, and to accept it, before stuffing it back into its box where it belonged.

A Saturday night, teatime with Mam and Sheila, then playtime in the lane, hopscotch, chasey, tag, and knocky-door-ginger. Then it's dark, and Mam calls us in and, as always, I see the tension in her face, and how she longs to delay the inevitable.

'Rosie, pet,' she says, dropping to her knees and holding my shoulders. 'Wouldn't do iz a favour, would ye?'

I look at her, my mouth tight, reluctant to speak.

'Just once more, pet?'

I stare at the floor, nod, dumbly.

'Thanks pet.' She pats my head.

Pulling on my outdoor boots, I try to think of nice things. Times when Dad is sober or has spent a night playing games with us. But those times are long gone.

It's proper dark by now and the walk to the Fountain feels like being summoned to the headmaster's study to get a belt across the hand for talking in class. Except this is much worse. I pass a couple of older kids mucking about by the side of the road. One of them looks over, sees where I'm headed and gives me a hopeful smile.

Pushing through the double doors, I can smell the beer, the smoke, the earthy stink of working men. A hand on the Taproom door. A gentle push and I'm inside, in time for a cheer from a group at the darts board.

Glancing around, I see the backs of legs, jackets slung over chairs, fingers pinging fag-ends across the floor, chairs scraping back, calls to the barman. And there he stands, six feet away, shirtsleeves rolled, dirty fingernails gripping a pint glass, his other hand turning a cigarette around and around as if performing a miniature circus trick.

'Jackie.' One of the men has seen me. He nods to my father, throws me a leering smile, his face locked into a permanent scowl.

I watch my dad's hand as the glass swings upwards, tips to his mouth, beer sliding into his throat like a liquefied snake. Then he leans through the throng of drinkers at the bar, slides the empty glass onto the counter, drops his hand, pauses.

Here it comes.

His head turns, eyes glistening, mouth open. 'Fuck's sake…'

A lurch forwards, fist swinging towards me.

'Jackie, man, for Christ's….'

But the objection goes unheeded and my father's knuckles catch the side of my face as I veer sideways striving to escape the full force of it. Ducking down, I swivel and grab for the still-open door.

'C'mere, ye fuckin'…'

And I'm gone, tearing back down the street towards home, thudding boots behind me, gaining, almost upon me. Then a drunken hand hooks my arm and I feel myself whirled around and tossed across the path onto a patch of grass.

'What've Ah fuckin' telt, ye…?'

He looms over me, swaying back and forth like a ship on a tumbling ocean, one foot already swinging backwards, ready for a hefty kick.

My legs lash out as his foot sails towards me, and as if by some miracle, the edge of my boot catches his, knocking him off balance.

Lying on my back, I see his head disappear from view, crash towards the ground and his other leg swinging upwards like a bizarre counter-balance. Long seconds drag past until with a sickening crunch, his head hits the pavement.

A face looms into view, staring down at me, its mouth wide open. The Scowler. He crouches down, puts his head to my father's chest, listens, pauses, straightens up. For a long moment, he looks right at me, his face a mixture of anger and shock. Then he laughs.

'Shouldn't've done that, lassie.' He stands up, looks back towards the Fountain, looks at me. 'Shouldn't have.' And then he's gone, striding back to the pub.

Slinking away from the body, I crawl into the shadow cast by someone's garden wall and watch my father, waiting for him to recover, to haul himself to his feet, to see me, to finish what he's started.

But he doesn't.

'Where's yer dad, pet?' says Mam, gazing past me down the lane.

'He's comin', I say, pushing past her.

The next morning, a couple of the neighbours have found the body and come running to tell Mam.

She hurries out, Sheila bounding after her like an eager dog, desperate to learn what new episode has so shocked the neighbours.

By the time I arrive, standing behind my sister, a crowd has gathered, someone kneels, utters sombre, gloom-ridden phrases, comforts Mam, shoos away the crowd, dishes out instructions that someone ought to, *Get those bairns away* before the police arrive.

And somewhere in the background, I catch sight of The Scowler, grinning at me.

12

We were halfway through breakfast when Inspector Walton arrived.

'Cup of coffee, Inspector?' said Sheila, cheerily.

'No thanks, pet,' he said, sliding into a chair. 'Ah've got news.' To me, he said, 'Our friend Mr Box has coughed to a variety of stolen property and illegal substances. But's he's saying nowt about the murders and claims the dead woman we found must've been left in that shed when he wasn't lookin.'

'But you've got evidence to tie him to the body?' I said.

'Ah'm hoping we will have. CID are on top on things, but so far there's no fingerprint evidence, or anything else for that matter, that links directly to Bernie Box. When we get hold of Charlie, Ah dare say it'll be a different matter.'

'So, this Charlie bloke's still on the loose?' said Sheila, hands on her hips. 'And where does that leave our Rosie?'

'Sheila, it's fine,' I said. 'The inspector knows what he's doing.'

'Bloody better do. Ah divvent want to be traipsin'

doon to the morgue to identify me sister's body anytime soon.' She stormed off into the back yard to put the bins out.

'She just cares about me, that's all,' I said. 'Not so long ago, I didn't think she gave two hoots, so…'

'Aye, death has a way of bringing folk together.'

'Cindy's still missing, then?'

He nodded. 'We're checking all known associates for Charlie Box. Anyone who might give him a place to hole up. Anywhere he might be hiding.'

'I thought you said he was still in London?'

He swallowed hard. 'Aye, well he is. As far as we know. But with his dad locked up, he might decide to come back.'

'Come back to take revenge?'

'Possibly.'

'You're not making this sound appealing, Mr Walton.'

'Vic.'

'What?'

'My name's Vic.'

'As in Victorious?'

'Ah hope so.' He tapped his fingers on the table. 'Ah'm putting a constable outside the house. For the next couple of days, at least.'

'Nights too?'

He nodded.

'And I suppose you're expecting me to stay at home all day long?'

'That's what Ah'd prefer.'

He left shortly afterwards, and Sheila and I spent the morning having a clear out of all Mam's things, in between checking to see what the dark-haired young copper was doing.

'Nice lookin lad, that,' observed Sheila. 'Ah could show him a thing or two.'

'And you a married woman, as well.'

'We can all dream, pet.'

I put down the box I'd been looking through. 'Is everything alright? With you and Bob?'

'How d'ye mean?'

'Well, you told me he didn't want you going out to work, but when I asked Bob about it…'

She sat down on the arm of the sofa. 'It hasn't all been plain sailin. He's always so busy, an' that. Always tired when he comes in from work.'

'Go on…'

She twiddled with her wedding ring, turning it around. 'Ah've been havin an affair.'

'Jesus, you what?'

'Don't say it like that, Rosie, it's not like we're a couple of fuckin' nuns, is it?'

'No, but…'

'No but nothin. Ye don't know what it's like.' She paused. 'Or maybe ye do…'

'Who is he?'

'He's not. Not anymore. It's over.'

'Alright then, who was he?'

'Called him Jimmy Milne. A fitter down at Swan Hunters on the late shift. Ah'd been down there to see about a secretarial job, an' bumped into him on the way out. We got talkin'. Within a couple of weeks, he was comin' up to mine after Bob left for work.'

'Cosy. When was this, exactly?'

'Four years ago.'

'And when did it stop?'

'The day Mam died.'

'Christ, Sheila.'

'Oh, don't. Ah've given meself enough grief about it.'

'And Bob doesn't know?'

'Course he doesn't know! Ah'm not that stupid.'

We sat in silence for a few minutes. Then I said, 'So you're going back to work, then?'

She giggled. 'Think Ah'd better, don't you?'

Sheila stayed for dinner and then I persuaded her to come shopping with me.

'What about that copper standin outside? What's he gan to say?'

'Won't say anything if he doesn't know, will he?'

She didn't need much persuading and ten minutes later we sneaked out the back door and ran down to the bus stop. It felt like we were teenagers again, running off to the pub behind Mam's back, swigging gin in the Percy Arms, pretending we were working women out to lunch.

'Where are we goin' first, then?' said Sheila as we hopped off the bus at the Haymarket.

'Need to get something for tea, go to the bank and then I want to pop into the Majestic.'

She grabbed my hand, yanking me backwards.

'The Majestic? What the fuck for?'

'I need to see Frankie Fenwick.'

'Oh, that's a good idea, let's ask him if he'd like to stab the both of us while we're on.'

'He's not going to stab anyone. The poor man's just lost his son.'

'Oh.' She sniffed. 'Ah forgot about that.'

Just before three o'clock, we sidled up to the main entrance of the Majestic, keeping our eyes peeled. I hadn't expected to see any cops around, but it didn't hurt to check. One of the bouncers lazed against the open doorway. He gave me a nod.

'Lookin for Fenwick?'

'Might be,' I said.

'Go on, then. Don't tell him Ah saw ye.'

I gave him a sly wink and hurried up the steps, pulling Sheila along behind me.

There were only a handful of punters in, dregs from the lunchtime session. Eddie was at the bar, urging two old guys to drink up and be on their way. He saw me approaching and suddenly became very animated.

'What ye doin' here? Frankie'll go nuts.'

'It's Frankie I want to see.'

'Oh. Right.' He picked up the empty glasses one of the old men had slid onto the bar and gave them a half-hearted wash in the sink. 'He'll be in his office.'

'Where's that?'

He nodded toward the other side of the room. 'Up the stairs as far as ye can go.'

'Thanks, pet. By the way, this is my little sister, Sheila.'

Sheila gave him a shy wave and we hurried across towards the stairs.

'Is that Eddie?' she said as we tramped up the steps.

'Yes, that's Eddie, and you're to keep your hands off him.'

The office was where he'd said it would be, the door standing open, light streaming in from a window on the side wall.

Frankie sat behind a wide mahogany desk, piles of letters and invoices on one side and a smaller pile in front of him. A pair of half-moon glasses perched on his nose. Looking up, he took them off and leaned back, twirling the spectacles between thumb and forefinger.

'Doing a bit of shopping, eh? Wish Ah could've come wi' ye — forget about this fuckin' place for a while.' His voice had a weary, disappointed note to it. The usual sneer had gone, and he looked as if he'd been awake for several days. Pushing his fingers through what remained of his hair, he gave me a sad sort of smile.

'Sorry to hear about your son,' I said, putting my bags down on the floor. 'Must be a difficult time for you.'

His teeth clenched and a hiss of breath emerged through thin lips. I guessed it took a bit of effort to keep the tears at bay, even for a so-called hard man like him.

'How's your pal the inspector?' he said.

'Alright, as far as I know.'

'Ah hear you're his new sidekick.'

'He's just trying to stop me from getting hurt, that's all,' I said. 'And catch whoever it is that's going around killing all these women.'

'And my son,' he muttered.

I felt my face flush. 'Of course.' I paused for a minute to get my thoughts in order. 'Did you hear about Jeanie Little?'

Fenwick's face wilted. 'Aye, Ah did.'

'You knew her?'

'She sang here a few times. Regular spot. Ah was expectin' her back last month. When she didn't show, Ah thought she must've got a better offer.'

'From another club owner, maybe?'

He looked at me, seemed to be sizing me up. 'How much d'ye know about that copper and his investigation?' he said, leaning forwards.

'It was me who found Jeanie, so I know about that Bernie Box feller and his son.'

He sighed. 'Young Charlie, Aye. Dangerous fucker, by all accounts.'

'Some folk would say the same about you, Mr Fenwick.'

He stared at me for a long moment, then laughed. 'Aye, I suppose they would.'

'And you know this Charlie?'

He shook his head. 'Never had the pleasure. Bernie keeps him well away from the Dunston depot. Even sent him to London for a while to stop him beatin' up folk.' He massaged the bridge of his nose. 'So, is this just a social call, or what…?'

'I've got questions.'

He waved at hand, indicating two chairs on our side of the desk. 'Make yourselves comfortable.' He glanced at Sheila.

'This is my sister,' I said. 'She's here for moral support.'

Sheila's eyes went like saucers, but she said nothing.

'Don't know if you're aware, but the night she disappeared, Julie made a phone call from here.'

Frankie sat up straighter. 'No, Ah didn't know that.'

'See, the police started out thinking this was about young women getting raped and murdered, but I think whoever Julie called that night, was *expecting* her to call and that whatever she said to that person is what got her killed. I think everything else is just…I don't know, almost incidental.'

He shook his head. 'Look pet, Ah appreciate ye're trying to find out what's going on, but Julie calling someone to tell them something that gets her killed…nah. Ye sound like one of those bloody Agatha Christie stories. Convoluted.'

'Oh, I suppose you're another one that likes Raymond bloody Chandler?'

'What?'

'Nothing. Look, is there anything about you or the Majestic that could benefit Bernie Box? Or his son, for that matter?'

Fenwick swivelled round on his chair, stared at a spot on the wall. 'We were mates, me and Bernie. Way back. Did everything together. Even went out with the same girl for a while. But we didn't want to work, ye see? Not like ordinary people. So, we started a business. Buying and selling. Anything we could get our hands on. Made a fair few quid knocking out black market fags an' scotch during the war. But Bernie wanted more. Wanted to get into racketeering and protection. Wanted my share of the cash to help him buy up a gambling den. But gambling wasn't for me and we fell out.'

'Was Bernie ever interested in your club? Or in the music business?'

'Bernie? Nah, he's tone deaf. Wouldn't know a

decent tune if it punched him in the gob.'

I frowned. This didn't seem to be getting me anywhere. 'Could Julie have known Bernie?'

He shrugged. 'Anything's possible in this town, but no. Can't see it.'

'You know Cindy's still missing?'

'Aye. And she's not even a singer, so that blows your clever theory out the water.'

'Yes, it does a bit.'

At this point Sheila shuffled forwards on her chair. 'Ah knew Julie.'

We both looked at her.

'Well, Ah did. An' like most folk, she didn't have a phone.'

'What's your point?' I said.

'Only that if she was planning to ring someone, she'd need to have the number written down somewhere, wouldn't she? Ah might be wrong, but Ah'm sure Ah saw her one time with a little brown telephone book.'

Frankie tapped a finger on a small black book on his desk. 'She's right there. Phone book. Probably in her handbag. That's what you lasses do, isn't it?'

I could've kicked myself. All the times I'd gone to make a call and taken out my own little book listing every number I needed. I could scarcely believe I'd never thought of it.

'We need to go.' I picked up my bags and pulled Sheila out of her chair. 'Thanks Mr Fenwick.'

'Not sure what ye're thanking me for, but any time pet.'

I stopped at the door and turned to look at him. 'Why'd you come and see me at the Prince of Wales?'

'Same reason Ah gave ye me business card. Ah know talent when Ah see it. And you've got it. In spades.'

I didn't know what to say to that, so I closed the door and followed Sheila downstairs.

Sheila wasn't happy about being rushed around. Why couldn't we have a nice gentle walk back to the Haymarket and get on the bus like normal people? But the police station was close enough to walk as far as I was concerned, and I didn't want to waste any more time. Cindy's life might be at stake.

On reception duty, the burly sergeant gave me a big smile. 'Glutton for punishment, eh?'

He went off to check if Walton was still in his office. He came back a minute later.

'Go on, pet, you know the way.'

Pulling Sheila along behind me, I wondered why coppers didn't call everyone 'madam' like they did in *Dixon of Dock Green*.

Halfway into his overcoat, Inspector Walton stopped when he saw us.

'What time d'ye call this?' He shook his head, as if I were an annoying child. 'Come on, then, make it quick.'

'Did you find Julie's telephone book?'

He gave me a weary sigh. 'Think we'd have noticed a bloody great phone directory sticking out of her handbag.'

'No, you daftie, I mean like this…' Rummaging in my bag, I pulled out my own little black book. 'A personal one. See?'

His brow creased up. 'Hmm. Ah don't recall one in her belongings. Hang on.' Slipping out of his coat, he threw it over the back of a chair and picked up a pile of folders. Extracting one, he leafed through it. 'Here…'

I moved closer to peer at the sheet in his hand.

Running a finger down the property list, Walton muttered, 'One small notebook in brown leather. That'll be it.' He looked up. 'Important, is it?'

I told him my theory about the number Julie had called from the Majestic.

He studied the list again. 'Like Ah say, Ah don't remember seeing it.' He glanced at the door. 'But Ah think Ah might know why.'

He went out and headed back along the passage, past the main entrance to a flight of stairs, Sheila and me scurrying along behind.

'We keep all that sort of stuff in the basement,' he said over his shoulder. Jumping the last few steps, he pushed through into a darkened room, walled with bare bricks and crammed with ceiling-high metallic shelving. Each section contained boxes and folders marked with handwritten numbers and file names. We squeezed between the two nearest sections of shelving, and made our way to the far end. Hauling a box from its location on the bottom shelf, Walton hefted it up onto his knee, then balanced one edge on the shelf.

'Grab that paper bag, will yer, Rosie?'

I grasped a brown paper bag that lay uppermost in the box and lifted it clear.

Shoving the box back into position, Walton took the bag to a small table that had been fastened to the wall in the corner. Emptying the contents, he sorted through the various items, pushing away a purse, a headscarf, a bundle of blood-stained clothing, a pair of shoes and a few personal items.

'It's not there.' He looked at me, his face grim. 'Right, then, Detective Robson, who do ye think might've been in charge of collecting this little lot?'

'Gingernut?'

'Also known as PC Thornton. Ah'll have his fuckin' bollocks for this.' He paused. 'By the way, aren't you meant to be confined to barracks?'

I glanced at Sheila. 'We have been, haven't we?'

'Tch.' To Sheila he said, 'I thought you were the sensible one. Take her home, and make sure she stays there this time.'

Sheila gave him a mock salute. 'Yes sir!'

'And ye might remind that idiot standing outside

your house that he's supposed to be on duty.'

We got back to Mam's about teatime. The young copper saw us approach and did a double take.

'How come ye're out here?'

'Sorry pet,' said Sheila, patting his cheek. 'We gave ye the slip.'

'Don't worry,' I said. 'We didn't tell Inspector Walton it was your fault.' I gave him a big smile and followed Sheila into the house.

'Are you going back up to yours?' I said, filling the kettle for tea.

'Suppose Ah should, shouldn't Ah? If Ah'm not there to make his tea, Bob'll think his throat's been cut.' She giggled, then realising what she'd said, muttered, 'Sorry pet, Ah didn't think.'

I made a pot of tea while Sheila collected her things together. 'I'll just have a cuppa then Ah'll be off.'

'What'd you think of your afternoon as a detective, then?'

She nodded thoughtfully. 'Ah think Ah'd enjoy going round asking questions an' that. Poking me nose in. Not so keen on looking at dead bodies, though.' She leaned back in her chair. 'So, who d'ye think's the killer?'

'Christ knows. But if we can track down that little phone book...' I shrugged. 'Every time I find out something new, I just seem to get further away from it. Maybe we'll never know.' I thought about this for a minute. 'It's got to be this Charlie Box bloke. But I don't have a clue why.'

'Well, Ah'm sure ye'll work it out, pet,' said Sheila, putting her coat back on.

I walked her to the door, and we stood there for a minute, looking up the street. The sky had clouded over, making it seem darker than it should've been for this early in the evening. Unusually for around here, there were no kids about and I had the oddest sensation that something was wrong.

'Where's that copper?' said Sheila, walking to the gate. She laughed. 'He's fucked off!'

Running down the path, I grabbed her sleeve and dragged her back into the house.

'What's the matter now?' she moaned, staring at me like I'd gone mad.

Pulling her inside, I shut the door and locked it. 'Maybe he has fucked off, but Walton wouldn't leave me with no protection. Not without telling me.'

'Ah'll check the back door,' she said, hurrying through to the kitchen. 'Should Ah check the back gate an'all?'

'No, leave it. Stay in here.'

She came back and we stood in the front room gazing out the window.

'I wish we had the phone on.'

'Ah could run down to the box?'

'No. Not until we know what's going on.'

'An' how're gan to know what's gannin on if we can't ring anyone?'

'I don't know.' I sat down and clasped my hands to keep them from shaking.

Sheila pulled back the net curtain and peered out. 'D'ye reckon someone's out there, waitin'?'

I opened my mouth, but nothing came out.

'It's not dark yet. They won't do anything while it's still daylight. Don't you think?'

As if in answer to her question, a splintering noise came from the back yard. Jumping up, I ran into the passage and stared out the kitchen window. The back gate lay in pieces in the yard and three men stood there, brandishing sticks, their faces hidden beneath black balaclavas.

'I think we're about to find out…'

13

The mob surged into the house like a river, crashing through the back door and throwing the kitchen table over. I backed away but they were too quick, grabbing my arms and pushing my face against the wall. Within seconds, a hood covered my head and my hands were yanked backwards and bound together. I heard Sheila yelp and guessed the same had been done to her.

'What do you want?' I said, my voice little more than a whimper.

An arm slid around my waist and fetid breath wafted over my bare neck. A mouth pushed in close to my ear.

'What Ah want is for ye to shut the fuck up.'

I'd no intention of making a fuss, so allowed him to lead me outside and across the yard. A cool breeze hit me as we moved into the back lane and a firm hand pushed me forwards. I stumbled against something hard. A metallic scraping noise and a thud reminded me of sound I'd heard before but for a moment I couldn't recall where. The hand pushed my head down and stumbling, my knee hit the side of a door. They were putting us into a van. That's where I'd heard the scraping noise—it was the sound the doors made as they slid open. Could this be a police van? Surely we weren't being kidnapped by a bunch of coppers?

Falling sideways, my head bumped against something soft. I knew immediately someone else was in the van, lying across the floor. Behind me, Sheila whined as she crawled in next to me. Then the door banged shut and a few seconds later I heard the engine start. The van pulled away with a jolt.

'Rosie? Are ye there?'

Sheila's voice, next me.

'Yes, I'm here, pet. It's alright.'

'Doesn't feel alright,' she muttered.

The constant jerking of the van from side to side didn't make it easy to move, but with a bit of wriggling around, I managed to get into a sitting position with my back against the cold metal of the vehicle.

The bag over my head seemed loose, so I gave it a shake, hoping it might drop off. I should've known it wouldn't be that easy.

'Sheila, where are your hands?'

'Behind me back, where'd ye think?'

'Roll over and see if you can pull this thing off my head.'

Not being able to see, made it difficult enough, but after a bit of to-ing and fro-ing, I felt her fingers grabbing at my head.

'Careful, you'll have my bloody eye out.'

She gave it a few tugs and eventually, I could see the pattern on her dress. Leaning towards Sheila, I pressed my face against her arm and dragged myself downward, forcing the bag upwards until it fell off.

'Oh, Christ.'

'What? What's happened?' Sheila's hooded face swivelled back and forth.

'I just found out where that copper went,' I muttered. Leaning towards her, I grabbed her hood between my teeth and dragged it free.

Sheila blinked in the dim light. 'Thank fuck for that — I thought I'd never see daylight again.'

'We're doing better than him, at least,' I said, nodding towards the young police officer who lay across the back of the van, hands and feet bound. 'Anyway, he's still breathing.'

Looking around, I realised this wasn't a police van, or at least not the type Walton and I had used. For a start, there was a partition separating us from the driver, whose dull voice we could hear over the roar of the engine.

'Ye think this is how they got Julie an' them?' said Sheila, her lower lip trembling.

'Could be.' I leaned back and listened, trying to gauge where we might be headed. We'd have had to come out onto the main road, and I had the vague sensation we'd veered right, the opposite direction to the city centre. I reasoned it'd be noisier too if we'd gone that way. Occasionally, another vehicle would pass by, but we seemed to be travelling more or less in a straight line, which suggested our destination was to the west and out of the city. And that couldn't be good.

'Show me your hands,' I said.

Sheila shoogled around. Her wrists were tied with some kind of thin rope. From the feel of my own wrists, I knew mine were the same. Without something sharp, we'd have no chance of freeing ourselves.

'Don't suppose you've got a dagger in your pocket?'

'No,' she said. 'Ah left it at home wi' me grapplin' hook.'

It seemed like there was nothing else we could do but wait and see what our captors had in store for us.

A few minutes later, the van slowed and turned sharp left. From the juddering sensations I supposed we must be on a rough track, no doubt heading for some lonely spot where we'd be raped and murdered.

The van came to a halt and I heard the front doors slide open. Then the side door hurtled back, and two men appeared, still wearing balaclavas.

'Where's yer bleedin' hoods?' demanded one.

'Don't matter,' said the other, 'they won't be needin' 'em where they're goin'.'

I hadn't noticed it before, but these two had London accents. Recalling what the inspector had said about Billy Hill, I considered this might be some sort of revenge attack by Bernie Box's southern pals. But that made no sense — why send a gang of yobs all the way from London just to kidnap two women Bernie had never met?

Dragging us out of the van onto the rough earth, I saw we'd stopped near an old barn. As I'd expected, we were miles from anywhere. Gazing around I noted the sky had darkened and the wind had turned cold. If we started screaming, no-one would hear us. Our prospects did not look good.

The two Cockney men half dragged, half carried us into the barn, while the other, clearly the leader, waved a wooden stick, a warning against the rashness of our risking a dash across the fields. Undoing a hefty padlock, he hauled one of the massive barn doors open and watched as his pals hustled us into the darkness. The leader stood guard while the other two went back and carried the unconscious policeman inside and laid him down on the floor.

Then the doors were hauled shut and we were left there, only a dull shaft of light from a hole in the roof to light our new prison. For a couple of minutes, we could hear the men outside talking, but then the van started up again and roared away. There was no way to tell if they'd all gone, or if one had stayed behind. I listened for a moment but couldn't hear any movement.

'They don't seem worried that our hoods are off,' said Sheila, a note of concern in her voice.

Looking around, I saw there were stacks of wooden packing cases here and there, a couple of chairs and some blankets and in one corner, a small table and a camping stove.

'Looks like someone's been living out here.' As soon as I'd said the words, I knew who that someone would be.

'Like who?' said Sheila.

'Oh, a tramp, probably,' I said, not wanting to give her anything else to worry about. It would only be a matter of time before the coordinator of this awful affair made himself known to us.

Looking at the unconscious copper, I decided it'd be better if we kept ourselves occupied. 'Here, give me a hand.'

I crossed to where the man lay and kneeling awkwardly, did my best to go through his pockets. A police whistle wouldn't be much good, but he might have some useful implement I could use to cut through our bonds.

Sheila crouched beside me and we pulled at the man's clothes in order to turn him over. Amazingly, a police truncheon had been left in the long pocket stitched to his trouser leg. Either the idiot kidnappers haven't noticed or thought he wouldn't be needing it.

Within a few minutes, we'd managed to go through all his pockets, but there wasn't anything of much use. Even the truncheon would be worthless if we couldn't free ourselves.

Looking at the packing cases, I manoeuvred myself into a standing position and stumbled over to investigate the nearest pile. Five boxes had been stacked close to one corner, but it wasn't until I reached them and noticed the space beyond, that I saw her.

Cindy sat propped against the wall, hands and feet tied and a dirty rag around her mouth. Her eyes grew wide on seeing me and a stifled sob escaped from behind the gag.

'Christ…'

'Is she…?' started Sheila, coming up behind me.

'Alive, thank God,' I said. 'Come on — we've got to get our hands free before they come back, or we'll all be fucked good and proper.'

Crouching down, I shoogled around and managed to pull Cindy's gag out of her mouth.

'Oh, Jezaz,' she gasped. 'You too?'

'Are ye okay, pet?' said Sheila, leaning towards her. 'Have they…Ah mean, are ye okay?'

'They've not touched iz yet, but they will,' she said, her eyes rimmed with tears. 'The main one, he told iz exactly what he's plannin'.' She shuddered. 'We're gan ter die.'

'No, we're bloody not,' I muttered. 'Not if I have anything to do with it.' I looked around the space again, searching for anything we could use as a cutting tool. The wooden cases next to Cindy had their corners reinforced with some kind of stiff material. What we needed was something sharp, or at least, metal.

'Have a look at those ones,' I said to Sheila, nodding to the far corner. I'll check these.' Leaning against the topmost case, I nudged it over until it fell onto the floor. The one underneath looked as if it had been partially opened, one of the nailed slats sticking up a little. Twisting round, I grappled with the end of the slat, trying to pull it upwards. At first, it refused to budge, but after a minute, I felt it give and then come loose. Pulling the end free, I moved sideways until the nails in the other end bent over. Turning back around, I peered into the case.

'Happy birthday, girls,' I muttered. Manoeuvring round so I could get my fingers into the gap, I pulled at the bottle nearest me. It had been securely packed with straw, but not so tightly to stop it moving. Giving it a quick wrench, I yanked it free.

'Irish whiskey?' said Sheila. 'Ye're not suggestin' we get pissed, are ye?'

'Might dull the pain,' I said, 'but no. Something a bit more practical than that.'

Still gripping the neck of the bottle in my fingers, I swung myself back and forwards to build up a bit of momentum, then let go the bottle and watched it fly through the air. It smashed against the wall with a satisfying crash. If there were anyone still outside, they'd have heard it for sure, but I was past caring.

Finding a suitable shard of glass earned me several cuts on my fingers, but I persevered. Eventually, I got hold of a triangular-shaped piece and set to work cutting the twine binding my sister's hands. Within a few minutes, she was free and swiftly set about cutting through mine and Cindy's bonds.

Hauling Cindy to her feet, we held her steady for a moment, her legs wobbling with the effort. She leaned against me, her face wet with tears.

'Ah thought Ah was a goner,' she said.

'You might still be, if we can't get out of here.' I looked at the barn doors. If they'd been padlocked again from the outside, I couldn't see any way of us getting through them. Giving them a tug, the doors persisted in staying shut. We'd have to find another way out.

'We could climb on each other's shoulders and get out through the roof,' said Sheila, gazing at the hole above us. 'Or maybe stack these crates up…?'

That wasn't a bad idea, but I was more concerned that we'd need a way of defending ourselves when the bad guys came back.

'We need to make weapons,' I said, rummaging around in the broken crate. In London, I'd seen a man get his face slashed with a broken bottle, the attacker using the broken neck of the bottle in his hand like a mini dagger. My fingers were sore where I'd cut them, and I had no desire to make matters worse. Pulling another whiskey bottle out of the crate, I wrapped a handful of straw around the neck. Shielding my eyes, I gave it a whack on the wall. Nothing happened at first, so I tried a few more times and on the fourth go, the bottle shattered, but so did the neck.

Two more bottles went the same way before I ended up with what I wanted — an intact bottle neck with a nice jagged edge.

'This is what we need,' I said, passing the weapon to Sheila.

'Not sure Ah want to stab anybody,' she said, eyeing the sharp edges.

'Let's hope we don't need them, then?' I said, as I set about making two more.

Soon we had one each and a pile of broken glass. 'Better get this cleared away so they won't see it,' I said, brushing at the glass with the side of my foot.

Using a bundle of straw to sweep away the debris, we managed to hide it behind the crates. Then, lifting the fallen crate back up to its original position, I surveyed the scene. So long as no-one looked closely, they'd never know.

Cindy came over and slid an arm around me. 'Just wanted to say thanks, pet.'

'Yes, well, you can thank me when we're all safely back in our own beds.' She gave me a coy smile, and I felt myself flush. 'Or wherever.'

We stood around for a while, unsure of what to do, but then the sound of a vehicle approaching provoked us into action. Placing the gag back around Cindy's mouth, we laid the ropes around her feet and wrists, so it looked as if she were still tied up. Sheila and I sat down by the crates with our hands, and our weapons, tucked behind us. Now all we could do was wait.

My watch had stopped at some point during our abduction, so we had no way of telling the time. As the distant hum of an engine came to my ears, it felt as if we'd been sitting on that cold floor for hours.

Tyres skidded to a halt outside. The engine stopped and two doors slammed shut. I heard a key in the padlock and the slap of metal against metal as the hasp was flung back.

14

The barn door slid back on its runners and two men appeared silhouetted against the moonlight. I guessed it must be close to midnight, though the time hardly mattered considering our situation.

The men stepped into the barn and peered around, as if checking nothing had changed. The smaller one brandished a gun, pointing it vaguely in our direction. The other had the butt of a revolver protruding out of his jacket. Both men still wore balaclavas, but one, from his stocky build and wide shoulders, was clearly the leader from earlier.

Raising one hand, he pulled the mask away and even though I'd guessed his identity, I couldn't help letting out a gasp. He had the same puckered maw, the same piggy little eyes, the same sneer.

'Ah see a hint of recognition, there, Rosie.' He laughed harshly. The man next to him joined in, as if not doing so might be judged disrespectful.

'Who is he?' hissed Sheila.

'Charlie Box. Frankie Fenwick's other son,' I said. 'The one who isn't dead.'

'That's funny, that—the one who isn't dead. Ye should be on stage.' He did a mock double-take.

'Oh, ye *are* on stage!'

'So what now,' I said, striving to keep the tremor out of my voice. 'More rape and murder?'

His face slid into a 'hurt' expression. 'Aw, pet. An' just when ye'd figured it all out, eh?'

'Wasn't difficult,' I said. 'You wanted revenge because you thought Frankie owed you something. Christ knows what — money, respect?'

'Respect? He shagged me mother and left me with that useless fat fuck Bernard Box. Why should Ah respect that? Ah could've been a proper son to him, instead of that fuckin' ugly twat Arnold. Ah could've learned the business. Ah could've helped him. But no. He chose to destroy me, so Ah'm gannin to destroy him. Everything he's got, his clubs, his bands, his record business, all the stuff he's lined up to make a shitload of money, it's all going down the fuckin' drain.'

He stood there shaking, his face almost scarlet with rage.

'I don't understand why you didn't tell him.'

He blinked. 'What?'

'Frankie doesn't know you're his son, does he?'

'So?'

'Well, don't you think it might've made a difference?'

'Oh aye, like he'd fuckin' care.'

'Maybe you should've given him the chance. Might've surprised you.'

'Shut yer face.'

'Why, so you can kill me?'

He let out a roar as if I'd stabbed him in the eye. 'Ye're just a fuckin' woman. What the hell would *you* know?'

Sheila nudged me. 'Don't wind him up, Rosie…'

'Too fuckin' late, pet. Ah'm already wound up and Ah'm goin' to take it out on you three bitches.' He began to unfasten his belt.

'Just me.'

'Ye what?' His hand paused, the belt half undone.

'Sheila and Cindy — they're not singers. Nothing to do with Frankie's music business. So just me.'

'Hah. Want ter be the hero, eh? Well ye can be, pet. An' see'n as ye're so keen, ye can go first.'

He yanked out his belt and walked towards me as he began to undo the buttons on his trousers.

Rolling sideways, I swung my arm in an arc, catching his leg with the broken bottle.

'Arrgh! Ye bitch!' He fell over, grasping at his injured leg.

The smaller man, lunged forwards, the gun aimed at my head, but Cindy had moved at the same time as me and rammed her weapon into his backside.

'She's fuckin' stabbed iz….' gasped the man, toppling on top of Charlie, his gun skittering across the floor, out of reach.

Even though they were both hurt, I knew it'd take more than a few leg wounds to put them out of action. Jumping up, I shouted to Sheila and Cindy to get out. They didn't need to be told twice and as they ran through the still-open doorway, I grabbed the gun and backed out into the night.

Outside, the moon gave us enough light to make out our immediate surroundings. Heading for the van, I pulled open the door.

'Damn. No keys.'

'Ah'll get them,' said Sheila, making for the barn.

'No, Charlie's got a gun, too. We need to get away before he pulls himself together.'

Even as I spoke, I saw a hand grasp the edge of the barn door.

'Now!'

Taking off towards the darkest part of the field, I shouted at the others to make for the hedge. If we could get out of sight, we'd have a chance. It was only then that I realised Cindy had nothing on her feet. Already they were bruised and cut and there was no option but to grab hold of her and half carry her across the ground.

'Leave iz, Ah'll manage,' she panted, wincing with pain.

'No you won't,' I said, dragging her along. 'Think you've been through enough without leaving you to that pair of bastards.'

'Ah'll make it up ter ye, pet,' she said, giving me

a wink.

Sheila ran ahead, and I could see we'd soon make the cover of the hedge. All we needed was time to get out of sight. But a shout from the barn, warned me Charlie had spotted us.

A shot rang out and Cindy fell heavily. I still had hold of the gun I'd picked up and though I had no desire to kill anyone, there didn't seem to be any other option. Raising the weapon, I aimed at a spot near Charlie's groin. There was a loud crack and the gun recoiled, sending a shooting pain through my arm. Peering through the darkness, I saw Charlie on the ground, clutching at himself. Whatever I'd hit, had made some impression. But the other man had emerged from the barn, running towards his injured boss.

'Come on, Cind,' I said, picking her up again.

'It hurts,' she murmured, limping along, blood pouring down her leg from the gash in her thigh.

'It'll hurt more if they catch us,' I said.

A minute later we reached the bushes and pushed through to the other side. At least now we were out of sight. If we followed the line of the hedge, we might get to the road. What happened after that, was anyone's guess.

Another shot rang out, whistling through the leaves above my head. I had one arm round Cindy and with Sheila supporting the other side, we dragged her over the rough ground.

'That's the last time Ah come back to yours, Rosie,' said Sheila, gasping with the effort of our load.

'Admit it — you love the excitement.'

She laughed hysterically and we hurried on, now only a few yards from the road. Reaching the corner of the field, I saw there was a gap in the hedge. It looked as if crossing over into the next field might be our only option. Staying on the road would leave us with no cover.

At that moment, the roar of an engine caught my attention and seconds later, the van hurtled up the track at the other side of the hedge and out onto the open road, its headlights blazing.

'Get down,' I yelled, pulling Cindy down with me.

We fell in a heap just as the van served into the field directly in front of us. For one long second, the lights lit us up like Blackpool Illuminations and I thought we'd had it for sure. But the van swerved into a gully and careered off at an angle.

'Quick,' I urged, hoisting Cindy to her feet again. Hobbling up to the gap, we struggled into the road just as another set of headlights caught us in its beam.

The car screeched to a halt and someone jumped out.

'What the hell ye's trying ter do, like?' the driver started.

'She's been shot,' I said, pointing to Cindy's leg. 'Those blokes are after us. Can you get us to a hospital?'

The man looked at me, saw Charlie's van skittering round in the field behind us and made a decision.

'Bloody Hell. Come on, then.' Taking Sheila's place, he grabbed Cindy and lifted her in the air, swinging her towards the passenger side of the car.

Piling into the vehicle, I shoved Cindy into the back with Sheila, then jumped into the front seat.

'Hey, Ah know you, don't Ah?' said the driver.

Christ, I thought, what a time to be recognised. 'Can you be quick, please?'

Glancing back, I saw Charlie had finally got his van turned around. Our saviour saw it too and throwing his car into the quickest three-point-turn I'd ever seen, roared off back towards Newcastle.

The driver's name turned out to be Gary and he'd been on his way home to Prudhoe after a night out with his girlfriend.

'Where are we, then?' I said.

'Just past Crawcrook. Bit out in the wilds, mind. Ye're lucky Ah was passin'. Mightn't have seen anyone else on this road all night.'

He had that right. If he hadn't appeared, we'd probably be dead by now. I sat back, hands in my lap, trying to take in everything we'd been through.

'We goin' to the RVI, are we?' said Sheila from the back seat. 'Cindy's bleedin' pretty bad.'

Gary sighed, but didn't comment on the blood oozing all over his nice leather seats.

It was almost one o'clock in the morning by the time the doctor had examined Cindy. He came back out to the waiting area where Sheila and I sat in silence. He looked at us for a moment, his face grim.

'I don't know what you young ladies have been up to, but I recognise a bullet wound when I see one.'

I'd told the nurses Cindy had tripped and fallen on steps. I looked up at him. I couldn't see any point trying to win him over. 'So what're you going to do about it?'

He made a clucking noise with his tongue. 'I'm afraid we've had to inform the police. I suggest you two stay put until they get here.' He gave us a stern look then stalked off down the corridor.

'Great,' said Sheila, 'that's all we need.' She looked around. Apart from a young mother with a vomiting child, the waiting area was empty. 'We'll be here all bloody night, now.'

'There's something I need to do.'

'What?'

'Come on,' I muttered. 'Before that bossy bugger comes back.'

Out in the street, it had turned very cold. Pulling my cardigan around myself, I glanced back at Sheila.

'Hurry up, can't you?'

'Still think we should've waited for the cops. At least if that mad bastard turns up, they could stop him blowin' holes in us.'

'I think he's got something more important to do than worry about coming after us just now.'

'Could've fooled me, pet. Ah really don't appreciate being kidnapped, tied up and dragged through bloody fields…'

Sheila continued in this vein for another few minutes until we reached the back lane. A couple of drunks lolled around at the far end, but otherwise it was deserted.

'What're we doin' here?' she said, staring at the toilets where I'd found Tracy's body.

'Not there,' I said. 'This way.' Taking her hand, I led her to the back door of the Majestic. The door stood half open, so I guessed they'd already started to shut up shop for the night.

Walking up the stairs, I could hear Judy Garland's voice. They were playing records, so at least someone would still be here.

At the bar, I saw Eddie, sorting out the night's takings at the till.

'Christ, what happened to yous two?'

'Tell you later. Is Frankie here?'

'Aye, he's upstairs.'

'Is anyone with him?'

'What? No, don't think so. What's goin' on, like?'

'Call the police. Inspector Walton if you can get hold of him. If not, anyone in uniform'll do.'

'What'll Ah tell them?'

I checked the gun was still in the pocket of my slacks. 'Tell them there's going to be a murder.'

15

The door to Frankie's office stood open. I paused for a moment, holding a finger up to warn Sheila.

A muffled groan came from inside. Sliding my feet carefully along the floor, I moved forwards. Gradually, the scene in the office came into view. Behind his desk, Frankie Fenwick had been tied to his chair. His face bled from several cuts around his eyes and reddish bruises showed his attacker had been here for some time.

In front of the desk, facing away from me, stood Charlie Box. In one hand, he held his gun and in the other a metal knuckleduster leaving no question about who'd been bashing Frankie's face. And in fact, no question about who was guilty of murder.

Lifting his head, Frankie saw me and couldn't help taking a sharp breath in. Charlie reacted instantly. He whirled round, the gun pointing straight at my heart.

'Sorry pet,' muttered Frankie. 'Ah've already told yer, Ah canna use another singer just now.'

'Oh, aye, fuckin' funny, that, eh?' said Charlie, the gun wavering wildly between me and his father, as if the holder were observing some bizarre tennis match.

'The cops are coming so you might as well give up now,' I said, in my best 'confident' voice.

'Aye, well, Ah think we've gone too far for that, haven't we?'

Glancing at Frankie, I detected the smallest of head shakes. From where I stood, I couldn't see where Sheila was, but I hoped she'd had the sense to stay out of sight.

Keeping my voice calm, I said, 'No, Charlie, it hasn't. Not yet.'

He laughed madly. 'No? Ye think not? That's a bloody good one, that, eh?' He turned to Frankie. 'What d'ye think, Dad? Is that a good one, or what?'

'Aye, that's a good one, Charlie,' said Frankie. His voice sounded as if he'd already accepted the fact he was about to die.

'No,' I said. 'Because you're not the one who killed those girls, are you?' I shrugged. 'Maybe you raped and tortured them, 'cos when it comes down to it, you're a sadistic bastard. But you didn't kill them.'

Charlie laughed, but any sense of humour had left him a long time ago. 'Hear that, Dad? She thinks Ah'm a sadistic bastard. Nice.'

Frankie's eyes seemed to be pleading with me. *Shut the fuck up, ye daft bitch*, they said. But I wasn't listening.

'Come on now, Charlie,' I said. 'Here you are

blaming old Frankie for all the problems in your life, and yet you haven't got the sense to stand up and admit that you're not actually capable of murdering anyone.'

'Ye think not?' He swapped the gun to his other hand, stuck out his arm, took a step towards me. 'Ye think bloody not, eh?' His hand shook but the look in his eyes gave me a jolt. Maybe I'd made a mistake. Maybe he *was* perfectly capable of killing someone. Me.

'No, you're not. And I'll tell you why.' I paused and hoped to Hell I was right. 'Because you're left-handed.'

He swallowed. Blinked. 'So what? Loads of people are left-handed.'

'But the person who murdered Tracy and Julie and Lizzy and Jeanie and Arnold...*that* person's right-handed.'

'Heh, that's a good one. Had me goin' for a minute there...' He licked his lips. 'An' who d'yer think this imaginary right-handed murderer might be, eh?'

'One of your mates. Someone who's got more balls than you. Apparently. Or put another way, someone who really does have the capability to take another person's life.' I paused again, feeling surer of myself. 'Someone who killed people long before he joined the police force.'

A noise on the stairs made me jump. Charlie's

hand jerked upwards and for one horrible moment I thought he might start shooting, but he didn't.

'Who's out there,' he shouted. 'Show yourself, or Ah'll blow this lass's head off.'

A hand appeared around the edge of the doorway, followed by a face.

Inspector Walton glanced at me. 'Ye alright, pet?'

'For the moment,' I said.

'Charlie Box, Ah'm arresting you for the murders—'

'It's not him,' I said. I kept looking straight at Charlie, holding his stare. Willing him to do the right thing.

'Rosie, this isn't the time for buggerin' about...' said Walton.

'I'm telling you, Vic. He's not the killer.'

Charlie's hand wavered. 'Looks like you're the one in charge, here, Rosie Robson,' he said, with a bitter laugh. 'Got it all worked out.' He nodded his head slowly. 'Ah'd have enjoyed bangin' you, pet. Even if Ah didn't get to cut your fuckin' throat.'

He raised the gun, pulled back the hammer and fired.

'Jezaz Christ...' Walton leaped forwards, throwing me to the ground.

Blood splatted across my face and someone behind me screamed. Looking up, I caught sight of Frankie Fenwick's face. He was crying.

In the kitchen behind the bar, Eddie soaked another handkerchief and wiped my face.

'Lucky he didn't kill ye,' he muttered.

'It wasn't Charlie Box who was doing the killing,' I said.

'Even so.'

Lifting my chin with a finger, he surveyed his handiwork. 'Ye'll do.' He leaned back on the table and shook his head. 'Christ. What a mess, eh?'

'At least Cindy's alright.'

He nodded. Smiled. 'Asked her to marry iz, ye know?'

'Oh.'

He laughed. 'Aye, right bloody dickhead I am. Seems like everybody else knew what she liked, expect me.'

'You'll find someone nice, Eddie. One day.'

'What? Someone like you?'

'Eddie. You know you can't marry the girl who knocked your nose sideways. Wouldn't be right.'

There was a knock at the door. Walton came in.

'Ah've sent your Sheila home with one of the WPCs. Think she's in shock.'

'I don't know—you'd be surprised what a Robson lass is capable of. She's surprised me over the last few weeks.' I took the handkerchief off Eddie and dabbed my mouth. 'What about that copper at the barn?'

'We've got a team heading over there. From your

directions it shouldn't be too hard to find.' He said nothing for a moment, then, 'Thornton's gone AWOL.'

'That'd be right,' I said.

'CID are on their way. Ah'll take ye home, if you're ready?' He nodded to Eddie. 'Need a lift?'

'No thanks, just live round the corner.' I knew this wasn't true, but guessed he'd had enough of policemen for one night.

Eddie picked up his jacket and went out, giving me a little wave.

Walton sat on the table. 'Always said ye were smarter than most of my plods.'

'Huh. If I'd been smarter, I'd have said something earlier.'

'No, you wouldn't. You were too happy doin' your Miss Marple act to think about the consequences. Besides, Ah think ye wanted some adventure.' He grinned, so I knew he wasn't serious.

'D'you think he's still after me?'

He thought about this. 'More likely he's gone on the run. Only an idiot would push his luck any further.'

We made the journey up to Mam's in silence. There didn't seem to be anything else to say. I knew there'd need to be some sort of interrogation to tie up all the loose ends. More importantly, there'd have to be an investigation into how a corrupt ex-soldier came to be accepted into the police force, though I guessed that might be an ongoing issue. Besides, having the police investigate themselves, didn't sound like a particularly sensible idea.

'Oh, shite,' I muttered. 'We've got no back door.'

Walton sighed. 'Right. Well, how about ye collect what ye need and ye can stay at mine?'

'What? Without a chaperone?'

'Aye, very funny. Charlie was right about that — ye should be on the stage.'

'How much did you hear?'

'Not all of it — too busy trying to work out how not to get you killed.'

We went into the house and I stood in the hallway for a moment, listening. A cold wind blew in through the space where the back door had been. The kitchen table lay in bits strewn across the floor. God knows what any potential buyer'd think if they came to look at the house.

'I'll just nip upstairs,' I said.

Walton nodded. 'Ah'll find something to block that hole up with, otherwise ye'll have all sorts in here, nicking stuff.'

Upstairs, I looked into my bedroom. It felt like ages since I'd been there, and yet it could only have been a few hours. Taking the gun out of my pocket, I slid it into the top drawer in amongst my underwear. Then picking up the clothes that I needed, stuffed them into a pillowcase. Maybe staying at the inspector's house wasn't such a bad thing. Might be quite nice, even. I knew Ricky was keen to persuade me into some sort of rekindled relationship with him, but I didn't want to go back to that. Musically, maybe, but I'd left his bed for good.

A noise downstairs brought me back to the present. Walking out onto the landing, I heard a thud. Probably Walton sorting out the back door.

'Vic?' I called. No answer. That alone should have told me there was something wrong. But instead, I called again, 'Hey, Vic—not making a mess, are you?'

A thud on the stair prompted me to look over the banister.

'Think it's about time me an' you 'ad a little talk.' Thornton peered up at me. 'Or else I could send your cop friend to a better place.' He waved a gun. 'Don't make me wait, girlie…'

Carefully, I walked down two steps onto the half landing. From here, I could launch myself into a dive, land right on top of him. But he was ex-army and he'd shoot me as soon as I moved an inch the wrong way.

'What do you want,' I said, walking slowly down towards him.

'What do I want, girl? What the fuck d'ye fink I want? You fucked fings up for me good an' proper, so now I'm goin' to fuck fings up for you.'

'Oh, right. As long as we're clear.'

I caught sight of Vic lying in the hallway, blood oozing from a cut on his head. Reaching the foot of the stairs, I stopped.

Thornton stepped back, waved the gun at me. 'In there.'

Looking down at the inspector, I thought I saw an eye twitch, but it must've been wishful thinking. Stepping over him, I walked slowly into the front room and waited.

Thornton stood in the doorway. 'Close the curtains. Don't want the bloody neighbours peerin' in do we?'

I did as he asked, glancing into the street, hoping someone might see, but even Ivy Paterson and her fool of a husband wouldn't be looking out of their windows at this time of night.

I turned to face him. 'What now?'

'Don't you know, girlie?' He waved the gun at me. 'Strip. Let's 'ave a look at your assets.'

As slowly as I dared, I began to undo my cardigan. 'How did you meet?'

'Yer what?'

'You and Charlie Box. How did you meet?'

'What's it matter?'

'I might want to write a book about it someday. Want to get my facts right.'

'Huh, Charlie said you was a fuckin' comedian.'

He sniffed, waited for me to slip out of the cardigan. 'London. He was working wiv Billy Hill same time as me.' He paused. 'Shoes.'

I kicked my shoes off. 'So, you were already bent before you joined the force?'

He laughed. 'Christ, you're priceless, you are. Don't you know nuffin?' He waved the gun at my blouse. I started to unbutton it.

'What d'you mean?'

He let out a long breath. 'Fuck's sake.' He watched me for a moment, then, 'What'd you fink? That coppers are all honest as the day is long? Well, I'll tell yer—they ain't. There's blokes like me in every force, all over the country, just waitin' for a chance to take advantage. You fink I'm the only one round 'ere? Fink I was able to do all this meself? I'll tell yer, you don't know the 'alf of it. An' anyway, what we're doin' is good for the country. Stops this bloody Government screwin' fings up all the bloody time. What this country needs is men wiv ideas. Men wiv a bit of gumption. Men like me.'

'To do what? Kill women?'

'To do what's necessary. I'm lucky cos killin' women is somefing I enjoy. An' if some stupid git like Charlie Box takes the rap for it, so much the better.'

I'd finished with the buttons, so slipped my blouse off. Thornton stared at my chest. 'So it was Charlie who got you to kill those women, and Mr

Fenwick's son?'

Thornton laughed. 'Funny fing is, at the beginning I thought he was right. You know, taking revenge on 'is dear old dad, an' that. But then it got stupid. He totally lost control.' He shook his head as if he were talking about a soldier who'd let his squad down.

'So it's you who's pulling all the strings. You that knows exactly what's going on?'

'Ain't you been listenin', girl? That fucker couldn't wipe 'is arse wivout my say so.'

'Oh? And what're you going to do when he tells the police the whole story?'

He laughed. 'Can't, can he? He's dead.'

I laughed, mimicking him. 'Who told you that?'

He paused. 'He's dead. Shot himself.'

I shook my head. 'No. It was Frankie Fenwick who got shot. Charlie's still very much alive.'

Thornton, wavered. 'No, no, no, you ain't gonna mess wiv me, girl. I'm the one that knows, not you.' But his voice faltered. He wasn't sure. Not any more.

'Maybe you should check, before you do anything else…'

His arm slid down to his side and he frowned. At that same moment, Inspector Walton grabbed the man's ankle and yanked it backwards. Thornton fell forward and caught his head on the sideboard. Before he had a chance to get up, I grabbed his gun and stepped over him.

'You'd better take this,' I said to Vic, who by now was on his knees.

'Nip down to the corner and call nine, nine, nine, will you?'

'It'd be a pleasure, Inspector.'

16

We never found out for sure who Julie and Tracy had called the nights they disappeared. It may have been Thornton but could just as easily have been another person in the so-called 'men with ideas' group Thornton had talked about. It was a scary thought, that the police force and other organisations could be rife with corruption, groups of people dedicated to taking what they wanted and to Hell with anyone else, but it also made a lot of sense. It explained some of the things that'd happened recently.

Walton found Julie's missing telephone book at Thornton's flat. He also found a list of names. Among them were those of the dead girls and Arnold Fenwick. Each one had a line drawn through it. But there were other names on the list too. Cindy's, Eddie's and mine. Frankie's name was the last one, with a question mark against it. It seemed Charlie Box really had wanted to wipe out everything his father had built up, but maybe he also wanted Frankie to live with that knowledge, to realise, somehow, that he was to blame. Even though he wasn't.

The phone number I'd found on the matchbook turned out to be for a knocking shop on Ridley Place. A few weeks later, the house was raided, though no arrests were made.

When things had calmed down a bit, some people came to view the house. A young couple who'd been living with the husband's parents and had finally saved up enough money to buy a place of their own. I didn't envy them, but like a dutiful daughter, I went through the motions, pointing out the advantages of living so close to the city, the friendly corner shop, the telephone box on the corner.

A week later, they put in an offer.

Ricky helped me find a flat on Westgate Road. I'd be sharing with another woman—a Marks and Spencer's cashier who I thought might have a drink problem. But it was a start. And though I'd agreed to re-join the band on a part-time basis, I'd also accepted a regular spot at the Majestic, courtesy of Frankie Fenwick, who, it seemed, now thought of himself as my new best friend. It wasn't ideal by any means, but it would be a living of sorts and would keep my finances in order until Sheila and I got the money from the sale of the house.

Getting things together for the move, I came across the gun in my top drawer and remembered there was still something else I needed to do.

Pushing through the double doors, I turned right and walked into the bar. Catching sight of John, I couldn't miss the sigh that escaped his lips.

'Rosie, pet, Ah don't think it's a good idea for ye to be in here.'

'Really, John? I think it's a very good idea.' I patted my coat pocket, checking the gun. Then scanning the dozen or so faces who'd turned to see what the interruption might be, I spied my objective.

The Scowler.

He stood at the far end of the bar, the only person in there who apparently had no curiosity about the newcomer.

'Hey, Fuckface.'

A low murmuring started up and a few of the men swung their heads to look over at the one man who seemed to be taking great pains to ignore me.

'Ah'm talkin' to you, shit-for-brains.' My legs began to wobble, and I shifted position, forcing my knees to stay still.

He turned towards me.

'Know yer name, eh?'

The murmuring stopped and it seemed that the whole place held its breath.

Draining his pint, Scowler thudded the glass onto the bar. 'What hev we got here? Fanny on a stick?'

I took a few steps towards him and the other men edged backwards as if this were the American West and something bad might be about to happen.

'Got a problem with women, have ye?'

He glared at me. 'Have ye forgotten, pet? No lasses in here. Men only.'

'Then why are *you* in here?' I said.

I heard a few whisperings along the lines of, '*Oh fuck*' and '*She's done it noo*', but none of them could bear to look away.

The Scowler stepped forwards. 'Hadaway back to yer mammy.'

'Too late. Me mam's dead.'

He cackled. 'Aye, pet. Life's a bitch.'

'Just answer me one question, and Ah'll go.' I moved closer, narrowing the space between us. He was so close I could smell his breath.

'What's this, Twenty Questions?'

'No, just the one. Why'd ye never tell the police that Ah killed me dad?'

'What?' He peered at me, twisted round, looked at John. 'What's she on about?'

John leaned across the bar. 'Her dad was Jackie Robson.'

I watched the Scowler's face. His eyes skidded around the room, as if searching for some long-lost piece from a half-remembered jigsaw. He stared at John. 'Jackie? Big Jackie?'

'Aye, man.' John waved a hand in my direction. 'That's his eldest. Rosie.'

The Scowler stared at me. 'You're little Rosie?'

His face seemed to light up for a second, then his mouth opened and closed. 'Oh Christ, aye. Huh.' He nodded.

'Ye do remember, then?'

He rubbed his face. 'Aye. Ah do. Came after ye, didn't he? Gave ye a right good smack across the head.' He mimed throwing a dart. 'Onehundredandeightyyyy!'

I nodded, my hand in my pocket, finger resting on the trigger guard.

'An' ye think ye killed him?' He laughed, scornfully. 'You? Stick Woman? Nah. He was pissed. Fell over. Just like that—smack! Mind, he always was a dopey bugger.'

I blinked. 'Ye saying it was his own fault?'

'Whey man, ye think a fuckin' bairn could fell a man? Divvent mek me laugh.'

'Ah was eleven.'

'Eleven, aye. And skinny.' His eyes ran up and down my body. 'Still are—Ah've seen bigger things in broth.' He sneered. 'No, maybe ye wanted to kill him pet. Maybe ye'd have loved to be responsible. But ye're not. Ye're just a skinny little lass. Jackie Robson's lass.'

'Then why...?' I shook my head, trying to clear the haze of this new information, wanting to ask, wanting to demand why this vile-looking man had haunted my dreams, why the thought of him revealing my secret had disturbed my sleep all these years. But now I saw what he'd seen, a grown man picking on a kid. What happened that night hadn't been down to me at all, it hadn't been my fault. There was no question for this man, this drunkard, to answer — there never had been.

Taking my hand out of my pocket, I wiped my eyes. 'I'm sorry. Made a mistake. I'd better go.'

He laughed. 'Got your posh accent back, then?'

A general sigh of relief went around the bar. Before it died away, I walked out.

In the street, I took the revolver out of my pocket. Christ knows what I thought I might do with it. I stared at the weapon, appreciated its weight. Then I dropped it down a drain.

The End

Book 2 in the Rosie Robson Murder Mystery series, 'Blood on the Tyne: Head Shots', is available now. Read an excerpt below:

Blood on the Tyne: Body Parts
A Note on the Text

Some of the Newcastle locations used in the story are real, others did exist but were demolished many years ago, such as Campbell Street, where Rosie's mother lived. Still more are figments of my imagination. Dunston Staiths is now a tourist attraction, though the collier ships are long gone. The police station in Byker was situated close to where the Byker Wall now stands, near Conyers Road. The Fountain pub was located at the corner of Rye Hill and Scotswood Road, close to where Newcastle Arena is now. Finally, several venues used the name The Majestic, but the one I had in mind was near the city centre. My version of the building bears no resemblance to the real one — there was no cobbled lane behind the building and no stairs leading to outside toilets. And of course, it was never owned by a bloke called Frankie Fenwick.

Billy Hill was a well-known London gangster. Needless to say, he wasn't mates with Charlie Box.

Geordie Glossary

Ah – *I: Ah'm gannin (I'm going)*
Iz – *me: Leave iz alone (Leave me alone)*
Doon – *Down: Tek it doon (Take it down)*
Divvent – *Don't/do not: Divvent touch iz (Don't touch me)*
Fatha – *Father/Dad*
Gan/gannin – *Go/going: Gan away/Ah'm gannin away (Go away/I'm going away)*
Hadaway – *Go away. Also used as a demonstration of disbelief: Hadaway an' shite. (You're talking rubbish)*
Tek - *Take*
Telt – *Told: Ah telt ye (I told you)*
Tomorrah - *Tomorrow*
Mek – *Make: Divvent mek iz angry (Don't make me angry)*

Excerpt from Book 2:
Blood on the Tyne: Head Shots

One night in September Lucy Clayton came into my life. She left it a few days later when someone put a bullet in her head.

It began innocently enough with an invitation to a dance. The tickets came by way of my barmaid friend, Cindy, who'd wangled herself two free vouchers and then fallen down the back steps at the club and put her ankle out. Commitments to Ricky and the band, as well as my new regular spot at the Majestic, restricted my free time, so I looked on the prospect of a night off as something to be cherished. And given that my current list of friends could be counted on one hand, it seemed like the perfect opportunity to cultivate an authentic social life. With only my drinks to pay for, I quickly ran out of excuses not to go.

Dragging our Sheila along for company ensured there'd be someone to talk to if the evening turned out dull. My sister's new resolution to return to work, and her need to 'get back into the swing of things' after all the trouble with Charlie Box and that bent copper, seemed reason enough—even her husband encouraged her to let her hair down a bit.

Catching the bus into Newcastle city centre

on a Saturday night, made it feel like old times again—two young women out on the town without a care in the world. Sheila seemed to be in a good mood, though hadn't entirely given up her whinging nature—she complained about her new shoes pinching all the way along Bridge Street, until I insisted she take them off. We reached our destination—the Oxford Galleries—and joined the queue to get in, chatting to a couple of Sheila's pals. Then Lucy turned up and squashed in front of us, telling the folks behind we'd kept her place.

That Saturday night was the first time I'd gone anywhere remotely exciting since moving into the new flat. It also happened to be the first time I met Lucy Clayton—a flighty blonde-haired school friend of our Sheila's, who had her heart set on becoming a glamour model and had already appeared in a handful of fashion magazines. Perhaps if I'd taken more interest in Lucy's conversation that night, instead of drinking too many gin and tonics, I might've noticed her slightly odd behaviour, or seen something of the rabbit-in-the-headlights look that Sheila remembered later, when we heard about the shooting.

I saw Lucy again a few days afterwards, during a rehearsal. The Davy Thomson Blues Band had lost their vocalist and rather than force them to cancel, Frankie Fenwick offered my services for their gig at the Majestic. I didn't mind, as they were a nice bunch of guys and I knew all the songs, and though it was an extra date to what I'd arranged with Frankie, I didn't like to turn work down.

We'd stumbled our way through the agreed song list during the afternoon and were about to take a break, when I noticed a familiar face hanging around at the back of the hall with a couple of the staff. Lucy's eyes were on me as she talked to Eddie the barman, pulling at his sleeve like a needy child. Eddie made a face at me and jerked his head at Lucy—a sign I took that she wanted to see me.

After retrieving my cardigan from the dressing room, I crossed the hall to the end of the bar where Eddie busied himself washing glasses, upending each one on a tea towel.

'Where'd that lass go?' I said, leaning over the bar.

Eddie gave me a wink and nodded towards the back door. 'Just nipped oot for a breath of air, pet. Said she'd be back in a minute, like.'

But Lucy never did come back and the next time I saw her face, it had been plastered across the *Evening Chronicle,* under the headline, *Newcastle Model Found Dead.*

I didn't know it then, but Lucy Clayton's life—and more importantly, her death—were destined to haunt me until I found the person responsible for her murder.

Moving into the flat on Westgate Road had been fun. My new best friend, Detective

Inspector Vic Walton, made it clear he wanted to be part of my life, and willingly ferried me up and down the road with bags of clothes, furniture and various odds and ends. Though I always felt relaxed in his company, I wasn't so sure about starting a relationship, and told him I had no intention of rushing into anything. But I liked him a lot and knew it would be pointless telling myself otherwise.

The flat stood on the corner of Westgate Road and Brighton Grove, only a ten-minute walk up the road from Mam's house. Above an empty shop, it had its own front door leading to the staircase and a passage through to the back of the building. A shared corner yard with the first house on Brighton Grove led onto a back lane. Though no palatial dwelling, it had plenty of space and lay far enough away from the city centre to give the impression, if not the reality, of a quiet domestic street.

The evening I went to look at it, the other tenant—a Marks and Spencer's cashier called Marnie—explained how her uncle owned the flat, and she didn't pay any rent so long as she shared with at least one other person who did. The previous girl had gone off to get married, taking most of the furniture in her room, but that posed no problem for me, as my sister had agreed to my taking anything I needed from Mam's house on Campbell Street.

Marnie seemed nice at our first meeting and gushed continually about the first-floor flat's potential, the local shops and the bus stop close to the front door. She took me through to the vacant room at the back of the house, showed me the small, but reasonable, bathroom, and the attic space above, which Marnie used as a junk room. I know you're not meant to jump into these sorts of things and that a second look might've revealed the room to be totally unsuitable, but with the sale at Campbell Street going ahead, I couldn't stay at Mam's much longer, so told Marnie it'd be perfect. We chatted away for another half an hour before she declared the room mine if I wanted it.

It wasn't until after moving in that I realised Marnie might have a drink problem—empty gin bottles piled up in the dustbin in the back yard on Sunday mornings told a sorry tale. But as she worked days and I'd be out singing at least three nights a week, I reasoned the two of us would rarely be at home at the same time, so it wouldn't be an issue.

Later, it did become an issue, but by then I had other things to worry about.

Three weeks after moving into the flat, I'd met Lucy at the Galleries. Seeing her again at the Majestic, I wondered what she'd wanted, but then rehearsals and the gig with the Blues Band on the Saturday, plus a show with Ricky and the lads at a Whitley Bay hotel the next day, put any thoughts of her out of my head.

On the Monday, I walked over to Sheila's for tea with her and Bob. The kids were pleased to see me—even Devil Boy, who'd finally stopped calling me Auntie Minger.

My sister had been down to an engineering firm near Swan Hunters for a job interview and I wanted to hear how she'd got on.

'So ye gan ter congratulate me, or what?' she said, wiping her son's mouth with a dish cloth.

'You got it, then?'

She nodded, grinning. 'Start next week.'

'About time,' said Bob, pouring gravy over his pork chop. 'Now we'll be able to pay for all those new dresses.'

Sheila rolled her eyes. 'Whey man Ah needed a new frock for the interview, didn't Ah?'

Bob chuckled. 'Ah'm only kiddin. Be good to have the extra money, though.'

We'd finished tea and were sitting listening to Bob tell us about a girl at work who'd got herself in the family way, when the letterbox rattled.

'Ah'll gerrit, Mam,' called Devil Boy, galloping down the stairs like a baby elephant.

A few seconds later he appeared in the living room doorway brandishing the *Evening Chronicle*, swinging it around his head like a medieval mace.

'Watch what ye're doin wi' that, boyo,' muttered Bob.

The child handed it over, then stuck a grubby hand out, pointing to the remains of the chocolate cake Sheila had made the day before.

'Away with ye, cheeky sod,' said Bob, giving him a playful shove. 'Ye've had a slice already.'

The boy pulled a face, then turned to Sheila, giving her his best 'sorrowful' look.

'Oh, he can have another one, can't he?' she said, reaching for the plate. 'We're celebratin.'

'God's sake, woman,' said Bob. 'If ye let him keep stuffin cake in his gob, he'll end up like Elsie Fisher's bairns.' He looked at me. 'A pair of dumplin's, those two. Ah think their ma must give them lard sandwiches to school.'

Sheila pursed her lips, then put the plate down. 'Sorry pet, But Ah think yer dad's right.'

Devil Boy grunted then stomped off, thumping up the stairs.

'He's just a bairn, Bob,' said Sheila, folding her arms.

'Aye,' said Bob, turning sideways on his chair to open the newspaper. 'An he'll be a *fat* bairn if ye don't say no to him occasionally.'

Sheila said nothing for a moment but let out long sigh.

Bob looked at her. 'What?'

She cocked her head in my direction. 'D'ye have to read at the table? We've got guests, ye know.'

Bob coughed. 'Guest. Singular. Aye, Ah know. But your Rosie doesn't mind, do ye, pet?' He winked at me and went back to reading the paper.

'It's fine,' I said, giving Sheila a conciliatory smile, but my sister wasn't looking at me. Her head tilted sideways to peer at the front page of the *Chronicle*. With a quick movement, she leaned forwards and grabbed the paper out of Bob's hands.

'What the hell ye doin, man?' said Bob.

Pushing plates aside, Sheila flattened out the newspaper on the table. 'Look.' Her hand lay across the paper underneath a black and white photograph.

Moving over so I could see, my eyes slid over the image and the headline, took in the sub-heading and a few phrases from the first paragraph.

'Jeezaz,' said Bob. 'It's that lassie ye went to school with, isn't it?'

'Lucy. Aye—we just saw her the other day.' Sheila had gone pale, a trembling hand at her mouth.

'You alright, love?' I said, touching her arm.

She nodded, staring at the image of a smiling Lucy Clayton. I recalled seeing the same photo in a fashion magazine—it showed Lucy standing in front of a posh-looking house, showing off a tweed two-piece countryside outfit.

'Her first proper job as a model, that,' said Sheila. 'Dead chuffed, she was.'

The three of us fell silent as we each read through the story. Sheila finished first and sat back, eyes glistening.

'Ah canna believe it.'

The following Friday I'd arranged to meet Vic for a drink after a gig at the Prince of Wales in Byker. Ricky and the lads were on good form and we'd added a few new songs to our set list, which went down well with the punters.

It'd gone ten-thirty when we finished our second set and as the lads began packing up the gear, I went to find Vic.

'Good gig, Rosie,' said a woman's voice, as I shoved my way through the crowd.

Turning, I found myself looking at Patsy, the young WPC who'd saved me from intruders in Vic's flat a few months earlier.

She pushed a hand through her short blonde hair and nodded towards the bar. 'Inspector Walton's through there.' Looking back at me, she added, 'Expect ye'll be wantin to chat. Etcetera.'

I felt my stomach tighten. 'Think I fancy him, do you?'

'He fancies you.'

'Takes two,' I said. 'And as it happens, we haven't got as far as 'etcetera' yet. So, feel free—I'll not stop you.' I waved a hand towards the bar.

She laughed a bit too heartily. 'No, ye're alright, pet. Wish Ah could say Ah had him wrapped around me finger, but it never really got started.'

Her eyes slid downwards. I saw her knuckles

tighten around the glass in her hand.

'Sorry,' I muttered. 'Didn't mean to tread on your toes.'

'No,' she said, a note of friction in her voice. 'Like Ah say, he's not interested in me. Not really.'

We stood looking at each other for an awkward moment, then I said, 'How's it going at work?'

She shrugged. 'Same old. When they change the law and give the lasses equal pay an a bit of responsibility, it'll be great.'

I squeezed her hand. 'Aye. Not as bad as it used to be, though—they've got women reading the news now.'

'Aye—one woman. An d'ye think it'll last?' She rolled her eyes. 'A gesture, that's what that is.'

I could tell she wasn't in the mood, so didn't bother arguing. 'Well. Nice to see you.'

Walking through into the main bar, I recalled my reactions when we'd first met—the notion that something had been going on with her and the inspector. The pub might be her local, in which case she'd every right to be there. Still, I couldn't help wondering if she'd come to see Vic. Shaking the thought out of my mind, I told myself not to be so daft. Besides, it wasn't as if me and Vic were an item.

A shroud of smoke hung like a misty blanket over our heads, making the atmosphere stuffy. One of the few non-smokers had wedged open the door to the toilets and outside, letting in fresh air, which helped. The crowd had thinned out, drifting off in twos and threes to look for drinking dens that wouldn't kick them out at half-past ten. Vic, and a few other men I recognised as police officers, stood around knocking back the dregs of their pints. Propping one elbow on the bar, Vic winked at me. 'Here she is—the star of the show.' Clicking his fingers at the barman, he mouthed something I couldn't hear.

'Fuck's sake, Vic,' grumbled the other man. 'Ah've called time, ye know?'

'Ah'll call time on you, if ye divvent look sharp.'

The barman shook his head. 'Aye, fine. But if Ah lose me licence...' Taking a wine glass off the rack above his head, he poured a gin and bitter lemon and passed it across the bar.

'Cheers, Gerry,' said Vic, taking the glass. 'Ah've always said ye're one of the good ones.'

We walked over to a quiet corner and leaned against the wall.

'Were you watching?'

He nodded. 'Most of the time, except when some fat bugger stood in front of me during the last bit.'

'Should've arrested him for loitering.'

He laughed. 'If only Ah could.'

The phone behind the bar rang and Vic's head turned towards it. I watched his smile fade as the landlord held out the instrument towards him.

'For you, Mr Walton,' he called.

The inspector sighed. 'Isn't it always.'

Watching him lean over the bar, I saw his face harden as he listened to the voice on the other end.

Finishing his drink, he walked across the room. 'Sorry, pet. Duty calls.'

'Fat man blocking your view, again?'

'Sadly, no.' Glancing over his shoulder, he lowered his voice. 'A woman's gone missin. From what they're tellin me, there could be a link to modelling.'

'Like Lucy Clayton?'

'Aye. Just like Lucy Clayton.'

I hope you enjoyed reading this book as much as I enjoyed writing it. Please take a few moments to leave a review on Amazon and/or Goodreads - it doesn't have to be much, just a few lines about why you liked (or didn't like) the book.

Colin Garrow

Other Books by this Author

Books for Adults

Black Witch Moon
Blood on the Tyne: Body Parts
Blood on the Tyne: Head Shots
Blood on the Tyne: Red Snow
Death on a Dirty Afternoon
A Long Cool Glass of Murder
The Jansson Tapes
Six Feet Under
No Cure for Death
Terminal Black
Crucial Black
The Watson Letters - Vol 1: Something Wicker This Way Comes
The Watson Letters - Vol 2: Not the 39 Steps
The Watson Letters - Vol 3: Curse of the Baskervilles
The Watson Letters - Vol 4: Revenge of the Hooded Claw
The Watson Letters - Vol 5: Murder on Mystery Island
The Watson Letters – Vol 6: The Huanting of Roderick Usher
How the World Turns (and Other Stories)
Girlfriend, Interrupted

Stage Plays

Love Song in Sixteen Bars
Towards the Inevitability of Catastrophe
The Body in the Bag

Non-Fiction

Writing: Ideas and Inspirations (or How to Make Things Up)

Novels for Children

The Demon of Devilgate Drive
The Curse of Calico Jack
The Axeman of Manslaughter Mansion
The Architect's Apprentice
Mortlake
The Devil's Porridge Gang
The Hounds of Hellerby Hall
The House That Wasn't There

Author's Note

Writing, as they say, is a solitary business and being an indie author is no different. However, indie authors are a supportive lot, and I've been lucky in forging some great friendships among the online writing community over the last few years, as well as gaining a lot of useful tips and ideas about the technical and marketing sides of self-publishing.

I'd like to say a special thank you to Jacky Dahlhaus for her editing skills, her advice on commas, and for reminding me that my knowledge of punctuation still has room to grow.

Colin Garrow
February 2020

About the Author

Colin Garrow grew up in a former mining town in Northumberland. He has worked in aprocessor androfessions including taxi driver, antiques dealer, drama facilitator, theatre director and fish processor, and has occasionally masqueraded as a pirate. All Colin's books are available as eBooks and most are also out in paperback, too. His short stories have appeared in several literary mags, including SN Review, Flash Fiction Magazine, Word Bohemia, Every Day Fiction, The Grind, A3 Review, 1,000 Words, Inkapture, and Scribble Magazine. He currently lives in a humble cottage in Northeast Scotland where he writes novels, stories, poems and the occasional song.

Connect with Me

(All Feedback Welcome)
mailto: hello@colingarrow.org

Websites:
http://colingarrow.org
https://colingarrowbooks.com
https://thewatsonletters.com

Twitter:
https://twitter.com/colingarrow

Facebook: https://www.facebook.com/colingarrowthewriter

Amazon Author Page:
http://www.amazon.com/ColinGarrow/e/B014Z5DZD4

Printed in Great Britain
by Amazon